OUR JOHN WILLIE

By the same author

Katie Mulholland
The Glass Virgin
The Dwelling Place
Our Kate
Feathers in the Fire
Pure as the Lily
The Mallen Girl
The Mallen Streak

OUR JOHN WILLIE

WILLIE

by Catherine Cookson

THE BOBBS-MERRILL COMPANY, INC.

INDIANAPOLIS / NEW YORK

OUR JOHN WILLIE

OUR JOHN WILLIE

1852

One

The water rushed at them. It was as if the floor of the pit had opened and the sea were pouring in. Davy Halladay couldn't believe it was water; even in the light of the swinging lamps the top of it still looked like the floor of the pit, because it was covered with coal dust; only the dead chilliness around his legs, then his thighs and now his waist told him it was water all right. He was yelling to his father, "Da! Da! Where's John Willie? Da! John Willie . . . he's gone."

His voice was almost lost amid that of others, men yelling directions as they grabbed at the pit props supporting the roof, while others clutched at the great rocks that the props supported.

"Da! Da! Aw! . . ."

The filthy water rushing into his mouth choked his next cry. As he lost his hold on a prop, the last thing he saw in the light of the only remaining lamp before being drawn into the melee of struggling bodies was his father's head going under the black scum. And then he was being borne forward, thrashing, fighting, gasping amid arms and legs and strange terrifying sounds, and he knew now he was about to die and go to hell, as Miss Peamarsh had said he would.

Twice within the last month Miss Peamarsh had prophesied that he would go to hell: first, when she had caught him red-handed stealing an egg; the second time, he should have known that her prophecy would come true, because she had said it on a Sunday.

It was when he pulled their John Willie through a gap in her wall, a gap she knew nothing about because it was hidden by brambles. He had only gone into her grounds to gather blackberries, for in the great massed tangle that had once been a garden, the bushes were laden with fruit that was going rotten. . . . And then he had seen her cow.

She kept only one cow, but everybody knew it gave more milk than she could swallow, so he had crept up to the animal and, putting the tin basin that he had brought for the berries underneath it, had stroked her teats. She had just turned her head and looked at him as if she were thankful he was relieving her, and he had laughed and said to John Willie, "Here, sup that up," although their John Willie couldn't hear him; nevertheless, he always spoke to him. Three times he half filled the bowl and John Willie drank the lot.

He'd always had the idea that had John Willie had the right food he wouldn't have continued to be deaf and dumb. He had the idea that the right food would have loosened something at the back of his tongue and in his ears, for he had never heard of rich people's children being deaf and dumb.

When Miss Peamarsh had come upon them suddenly, he hadn't dropped the bowl and run; he had stood with it gripped tight in both hands while she glared down on him. She hadn't spoken for a long time, a full minute, and then she had said, "You'll go to hell, boy; you'll go to hell, and he along with you." She had pointed to John Willie.

She had stared a long time at John Willie, and he at her. People always stared at John Willie; his eyes seemed to fascinate them. He had beautiful eyes, had John Willie, like a doe's.

. . . God! God Almighty! God Almighty! Don't let me go to hell. He was dying. Da! Da! John Willie! . . .

But instead of his body being drawn downward, he felt it being dragged clear of the cold swirling water. Something had caught hold of his hair.

When the water gushed from his mouth he gabbled and yelled out against the mixture of pains he was suffering: the rock as it scraped his bare legs and the front of his body, and his hair that was being torn from his head. . . . And then he was clear of the water, lying flat on his face, gasping, groaning, crying. He felt hands moving over him, and it was some time before he realized whose hands they were. Then with a heave he turned onto his side and groped at the hands in the darkness. His own quickly traveled up the arms to the face and head, and now he spluttered as he cried, "John Willie! Oh, John Willie!"

Since John Willie was a small child he had been in the habit of passing his hands over Davy's face, very like a blind person might do. Often Davy would be awakened from much needed sleep by this strange brother of his stroking his hair or tracing the outline of his nose and mouth with his finger. And this was how Davy now recognized John Willie in the darkness. And he recognized him also, not only from his face—

the thin, fleshless face that held the over-large eye
sockets—but from his hair; even though now it was
wet and clogged with coal dust, here and there it re-
tained its silkiness. And then of course there was its
length. If only his body had grown at the same rate
as his hair, his brother, Davy knew, would have been
a giant, not an undersized deaf-mute, not "Halladay's
idiot," as he was called by many.

But Davy knew that John Willie was no idiot. Behind
the silence of his tongue and the deafness of his ears
there was a knowing. But it was only he himself who
seemed to recognize the knowing; even his father
looked upon his younger son as an idiot, not simply
because he was unable to communicate as an ordinary
boy would, but because he was puny in strength.

At ten years old John Willie should have been able
to earn a shilling a day down the pit. Boys of his age
did horses' work; where the roofs were too low to
allow for the passage of the pit ponies, the boys were
harnessed with an iron chain between their legs to the
bogies and, going on all fours, dragged them through
the low passages. But John Willie was no good for that
kind of work; he was no good for anything, his father
said.

Although John Willie came down the pit with his
father and Davy, he wasn't on the payroll; he was allowed to come down with them by courtesy of the
butty, and this had come about only through the insist-
ence of Davy, not of his father. Davy had dared to
stand up to his father and say he wouldn't go down
unless he could take John Willie along with him, for
to leave him up above meant leaving him to the mercy
of the villagers. Some were all right toward him, but
others, those who were apt to believe in omens and
signs, pelted him whenever he crossed their path.

Mrs. Coxon's lot were the worst. There were ten Coxons, and whenever possible they would make sport of John Willie. It was their Sunday game, the only day in the week when they could play, when they weren't working in the fields, or down the mine, and if there wasn't much to do they hunted out John Willie and, making a circle round him, pushed him from one to the other.

His da and Mr. Coxon had had a stand-up fight one Sunday. That was the only time Davy had really been proud of his da, for on that day his da had defended John Willie with his fists for the first time.

But now where was his da? And where was he? Where were they? Somewhere just above the water-line on a shelf in an old working pit, likely. He tried to think. He couldn't remember any passage going off into an old working pit with a shelf as high as this.

He was clinging as tightly to John Willie now as John Willie was clinging to him. He was experiencing fear as he had never known it before—well, not since his seventh birthday, the day on which his father had first brought him down below. The only thing that remained of that memory was the stupefying tiredness on him at the end of twelve hours of picking up pieces of coal and carrying them to a corf, which had appeared to him then like a gigantic shopping basket. He couldn't remember how many he filled that day; he only remembered the renewed terror that wiped away the great weariness when he entered the iron bucket-like structure and was hauled up into the world again, the world that although dark appeared bright compared with the blackness of the pit.

But this fear on him now was taking him not into the past but into the future, the short future in which lay death, death by drowning in the water he couldn't see, only feel lapping now about his feet; and if not that way, by starvation and cold. Both their bodies, although pressed close, were shivering with the cold. Like the fear, it was a kind of cold he hadn't experienced before.

He heard the human sound coming, not from the main rolley way along which the water was rushing, but from somewhere along the ledge on which they were crouched. He stilled the chattering of his teeth and listened. When the groan came for the second time he pressed John Willie from him; then going on his hands and knees toward the sound, he called, "Hie there! Who is it? Hie there!"

There was a gasp, a gurgling in the throat; then a voice said, "Bill, Bill Cartwright. Who's you?"

"Davy Halladay and . . . and our John Willie."

"Aw, Davy lad, you . . . you all right?"

"Aye, Mr. Cartwright. How's you?"

"I'm just trying to find out, lad. No bones broken that I can feel. Sodden wet and cold to the bone, but . . . but no . . . no bones broken. I must have passed out. Aye, that's what I must have done, passed out. . . . Any more along o' you?"

"No, Mr. Cartwright."

"Aw, well, God help them wherever they are. And God help us, lad. Here, hold out your hand. Aye . . . aye, that's better; I've got it. And that's John Willie with you, is it?"

"Aye, he's with me. He . . . he pulled me out of the water."

"Well now, that's funny, I seem to remember somebody trying to tug me out an' all, nearly tore the hair out of me head, but it was the weight of me, an' they let go of me again. But it did one thing: it turned me up this drift. An' you know something, lad? If I'm not mistaken I think I know this drift. But how to tell exactly? . . . Oh God! for a light."

"Will . . . will they ever get at us, Mr. Cartwright?"

The old miner hesitated some seconds before answering. "Not along the main road, lad; not along the main road. Any of them that was taken along that way, well, they're with the Almighty at this moment, that's a sure thing. . . . Now, now, lad, stop thy shakin' . . . ."

"It's . . . it's just the wet, Mr. Cartwright, just the wet."

"Aye, lad, it's just the wet. . . . And John Willie, poor John Willie, I wonder how he's takin' it? Aw, there you are, lad. . . . I've got his arm. . . . Funny, Davy, he's not shakin' half as much as we are; deaf, dumb, an' now blind as we all be. Anyway, you know what they say, lad. Keep on diggin', an' if you trust in God you'll soon came to the divil. . . . Now let me think. We were all in the main drift, weren't we? . . . And the shift goin' out from number four met up with us, didn't they?"

"Aye, they did."

"How many would that be? Forty, forty-five? Aye, forty-five, 'cos as I remember there were no pony lads—they hadn't got down that far yet—just the bairns that were released from the bogies. There was eight of ours; likely the same among their lot. Anyway, it doesn't matter so much about the numbers. What I'm tryin' to work out is which face they came from. I was tired at the time an' wasn't thinkin'. If it was Harry Lamb's lot, we would have been near the bottom of the road and the cage; but had it been him he would have hailed me; he always does, does Harry. No . . . I don't remember being hailed, so it must have been Peter Talbot's crew comin' from the Bolton Slip. And as you know, the Slip was not so far from our face; goes off to the left, when you're goin' in-bye, and to the right if you're goin' toward the bottom and the cage.

"Now, boy, let me think, and think again. The water came at us just after we were joined by Talbot's lot. What happened after that I'm not very clear about; we could have been swept for a mile down the roadway, or we could have gone round in a whirlpool. It seemed like that at the time—we were all goin' round in a whirlpool—but what strikes me now is that you and me and the boy here were swept out of the mainstream and up a drift. . . . Now which drift?"

"It couldn't've been the drifts near the face, 'cos three of them are blocked off."

"Aye, boy, there are three blocked off. An' that's interestin'. Why were they blocked off? All because of falls, heavy 'uns at that. An' not only falls, but the Fellburn Dip was flooded around ten years ago. Seventeen men met their end that day, but twice that number were saved. They got out through an adit. That's what makes them blocked drifts interestin'."

". . . An adit? What's an adit, Mr. Cartwright? Never heard that afore."

"Another kind of drift, lad, that's all; a drift cut into the hillside like a drain. An' that's what it is, a drain to take the top water away. An' by God! there was some top water in the Fellburn Dip. It was another of their follies, the masters' follies. Every shaft they sunk they went deeper. But now, lad, if God is good and we've been washed up on a road leading to the Fellburn Dip, we might see daylight yet."

"Do you think so, Mr. Cartwright?"

"I do, lad, I do. . . . But aw begod! what I'd give for a light. Anyway, if we can make our way along this flank, I'll know within a short while if I'm right or wrong. Get on your hands and knees, lad, and get your brother to do the same. Keep close to me. Now here we go!"

Davy quickly signaled to John Willie now by rapping his knuckles sharply against the boy's knees and then his hands, lastly pressing him on the back, and John Willie, answering the sign language as another would a voice, quickly got onto all fours and followed his brother.

It was soon evident to Davy that the ledge they were crawling along was going steeply uphill and widening at the same time.

The old miner had said nothing, and they must have crawled for almost five minutes before he stopped. Davy felt him rise to his feet, and when he went to follow suit the old man said harshly, "Bide where you are. I'm going on a bit by meself. Now bide where you are."

Davy swallowed deeply and only stopped himself from begging, "Let's come along of you, Mr. Cartwright; don't leave us alone here, not in this blackness." But he knew that the old man would never purposely leave them alone in the blackness, and so he held his tongue and listened intently.

For a few seconds there was the sound of Bill Cartwright's boots scraping the stone; then the silence became as heavy as the blackness. As he put his hand backward and squeezed John Willie's arm, as much in an effort to reassure himself as the boy, it came to him that he had entered the world in which his brother lived, the world of deep silence, and the compassion this knowledge aroused conquered his fear for a moment, and he drew the boy close to him and held him tightly. And John Willie touched his face with his fingers in the reassuring gesture that was peculiar to him.

"Lad! Lad!" The voice was loud and clear and

seemed to come not from in front of them but from above them.

"Yes, Mr. Cartwright?" Davy scurried to his feet, pulling John Willie with him, and turned his gaze into the blackness above him from where the voice came.

"We are in the Fellburn Dip, lad," Mr. Cartwright emphasized. "I've found the very place that I shored up twelve, nay fourteen years ago. The shaft wall crumbled along here, and me and Ted Connor and Ned Maguire put in the backing deals to hold it up. . . . Where we've just come along was the new road they made in-bye. Now listen, lad. Put out your hand and you'll feel the wall; move slowly along it; then you'll come to a dead end, a pile of rubble. Climb up there and I'll be waitin' for you."

With his heart beating fast Davy did as he was directed, and in a short distance he came up against a sloping bank. Gripping John Willie's wrist now, he climbed upward, pulling the boy after him until a groping hand found his collar and they were both hauled up and over and to the feet of Mr. Cartwright.

They were standing together now, the three of them touching one another, and the feeling of excitement was like a current passing through them; so strong was it that it melted the icy fear around Davy's heart and eased the trembling of his shivering body.

"Now I've got to put me thinkin' cap on, lad." Mr. Cartwright's voice had sunk to a whisper as if he were afraid of being overheard. "If I could remember the plan of this part it would lead us straight out into the hillside, but there are roads goin' off here and there, and you know in the darkness a man can go round in circles until he gets dizzy. But, anyway, we'll ask God to guide us, you and me. He's brought us this far, so He must know what He's up to."

There was a pause before he spoke again. "Now I'll have to feel every foot of the way. I want you to grab onto the back of me belt here, an' should I slip, hang on for dear life, lad, for we might or might not have only falls of stone to contend with but clefts in the floor. I've seen clefts big enough to swallow a cart and horse after the water's been through. . . . Can you pass it on to the youngster to do the same, to hang onto your belt?"

"Aye, Mr. Cartwright, he'll hang on."

Davy now took John Willie's hand and passed it over his belt, then pressed his own hand tight down on it, indicating that he should grip it. This done, there was another silence before the old man said, "Come on, come on, lad, we'll make a start."

And so they started. Like three blind beings they groped their way step by step through the impenetrable blackness, a blackness that was so heavy it weighed on them. Davy wasn't used to such blackness. Although he had been down the pit for most of his life, the darkness had always been relieved by a glimmer from a lamp. He had never been as unfortunate as the apprentice boys, the name they gave to the children from the workhouse. These were made to sit in total blackness for twelve hours at a stretch, opening the air doors to let the men through. And God help them if the keeker found that they hadn't closed the doors immediately, for they'd be kicked and punched black and blue, then left alone in the blackness again.

Once more they were going upward, and now the old miner exclaimed on a high note of excitement, "We're comin' to the junction, lad. Yes, we are that. Feel . . . feel along here; there's a road going off in-bye. Keep close; follow me."

They hadn't gone many yards ahead when again the old man exclaimed, "If I remember rightly there's four roads besides the main one. God! God yes! I remember, an' from where we are I tumble we're in the main passage, but there's one thing certain: this one won't lead to the hillside, only to a blank face. Now there's two roads going in-bye at yon side and these two here. Now, now, let me think . . . which of them did they turn into the drain?"

Again there was silence, the dark, thick silence. John Willie sidled closer to Davy, and Davy put his arm around his shoulders, and although both their bodies were trembling, Davy knew that he was sweating now.

"I'm damned if I can remember which."

The words were like the voice of doom, and Davy said softly, "Where will the other three lead, Mr. Cartwright?"

"Dead ends, lad. Water in some where the grade goes down, falls in others. The props were rotten years ago; they'll be mush now."

"Well, we could try one after the other."

"That sounds sensible, lad."

Davy knew that Mr. Cartwright had turned and was facing him, for he could feel the thin warmth of his breath, and he waited in the pause the old man made until he spoke again, saying, "But, lad, we're wet, we're cold, we're hungry, and if you're like me you're very tired, and in any one of these passages we could go on for miles if we don't come up against water or a fall. You know yourself how long the road was back there, from the bucket to the face, two and a half miles if an inch, an' these roads were no less. . . . Blast the pit, I say."

Davy felt the old man turn away from him, and his voice reechoed round the walls as he cried, "This one should have been condemned years ago; but no, they wanted their last drop of blood. The whole county's riddled with pits now. The coal kingdom, they call the Tyne. Aye, the coal kingdom. Aye, the kingdom of slaves, the kingdom of the blind, the kingdom of long everlasting night, the . . ."

"Mr. Cartwright! Mr. Cartwright!" Davy gripped the old man's arm, and his voice was urgent and his tone was not without fear as he cried, "Don't go on, Mr. Cartwright, you'll . . . you'll wear yourself out. I . . . I tell you what. You stay here with John Willie; sit yourself down an' rest, and I'll take the first road and see where it leads."

"You'll do nowt of the sort, lad. Where one goes we all go. Come on, we're at the beginning of this one, so up it we'll go."

They went up the first road. They must have walked and crawled and stumbled for a full hour before they came to a blank wall of coal and stone, and as their hands groped over it from end to end they said nothing.

The old miner, taking the lead once again, led the way back, and when eventually they reached the junction they sat down on the damp uneven floor, and although they didn't know it, they had all adopted the same attitude: knees up, forearms resting on them, spine bent, and head hanging in despondency.

It was John Willie who broke the silence. He broke it with his usual sound, the only sound he ever made, "Huh." The sound had so many inflections, so many shades, that it had become almost a meaningful language to Davy; but now it seemed to be trying to express something different. Three times he repeated it, and, as Davy caught hold of his brother's hand to reassure him and at the same time to assuage the new fear in himself, the old man cried with weary irritation, "Stop him doin' that, Davy. He's barkin' like a dog."

Yes . . . yes, that's what the sound was like, the whoof-whoof of a dog; yes, the huh! did represent a bark, and he realized that John Willie was reminding him that Snuffy, their old collie dog, was back there in the yard, chained up, alone, as alone as they were now. In his own way he was telling him that he must make another effort to get out.

He rose to his feet quickly, saying, "Look, Mr. Cartwright, now just you stay put alongside of John Willie. Give him your hand if you will—it'll save him from being frightened—an' I'll go along this other road. I'm not tired, I'm not really, and I'm used to trampin', you know I am. I tramp the fells every Sunday, miles and miles. . . . I'm not tired."

Somewhat to his surprise, the old man now made no protest, and Davy bent down and tugged John Willie along the floor to Mr. Cartwright's side; then he slowly patted the back of his brother's hand three times, and for answer John Willie said, "Huh!" But it wasn't like a bark this time.

It was all right saying you would go on alone, but actually doing it was, Davy found, a different matter. He hadn't gone many yards along the passage when fear hit him like a great wave from the sea, and like a wave it upset his stomach and made him retch. After he had brought up the oily coal-dust-filled water from his lungs he leaned against the wall, gulping at the heavy, foul air, and listened for some sound from the junction, a call from Mr. Cartwright telling him to come back. But there was nothing. It was with despair that he thought the old man was past caring.

He must have walked about a mile, his hands grasping at crumbling pit props and groping at the wall beyond them, and with each step tentatively feeling the floor beneath his feet, when, without any warning, he fell, not onto the hard stone floor but into water once again.

Gasping, choking, he flayed about until he brought his head above the surface, and he was about to yell out in panic when he found that his feet were on firm ground and that the water just came to his shoulders. His outstretched hands touched rock and he clawed wildly at it and pulled himself upward. Then, after reaching out to feel the wall, he recognized that he wasn't on the same road from which he had fallen into the pool, but in a narrow passage. He had come out on the other side of the water. But where was he now? He stood, his arms hugging his dripping body, and rocked himself as he fought against the turmoil of fear and indecision in his mind. This passage seemed too narrow to lead anywhere. But to get back to the other side he'd have to go into the water again. He couldn't do that; he couldn't. He'd just need to slip in the water and all sense of direction would be gone again.

He dropped onto his hands and knees now and groped wildly about him. His outstretched hands could touch each crumbling wall. But the floor was comparatively even, and it sloped gently away from him. He crawled slowly forward and felt safer on his hands and knees. Feeling every inch of the way, he had covered what he imagined was a third of a mile when of a sudden he stopped. What was it? There was something different about the blackness—not that he could see anything. No, the difference was the air. He took in a deep breath. Yes, it was the air: it was fresher, not so weighed down with the acrid smell of mold and decay.

He crawled on again, more quickly now, and then

he actually cried out in sheer frustration and anger as his hands came up against a seemingly blank wall. But when he groped along it he found that it turned, and he was in another passage, and there, there in the far, far distance he saw something that looked to him like a glimpse of heaven. It was a faint glow of light. *It was, it was. It was light, daylight.*

He got to his feet and only just stopped himself from running, cautioning himself to go steady, for there could still be drops, or another feeder, like the pool he had recently fallen into.

The light was still a long way off, but it was a light, and as he moved nearer to it, walking reverently now like one approaching a holy place, he began to experience a feeling of elation, but it turned to black disappointment when he realized the light wasn't coming from a hole in the hillside, but was filtering down from a shaft high up in the rock.

When he stood below the shaft and looked up the long, narrow cleft cut through strata of sandstone and coal, he shook his head from side to side. This was an old ventilation shaft, or perhaps a bore hole down which they used to drop the plugs to stop the flow of water when the pumps or the dams couldn't handle all the inrush. It must have been bored by donkeys years ago, for the light at the top was diffused by an overgrowth of greenery of some kind. But no matter, it would come out on the fells, or a hillside, and he had only to yell hard enough to make himself heard.

"Hie there! Hie there!" He paused and listened to the sound of his voice spiraling up the tunnel. "H . . . hie there! H . . . hie there!"

His hands cupping his mouth, he called. Again he called, and again and again. He called until his throat was sore; he called until he was tired and had to rest.

He called until the light began to fade and he knew that night was upon him and soon he'd be in complete darkness again. Almost in a frenzy now he began to yell. "Hie there! Help! Help! Anybody there? Hie there! Hie there!"

The light became weaker, but still he called, and when it disappeared completely he still kept on calling at intervals. It became sort of company to hear the sound of his own voice. He kept on calling until his strength gave out and he dropped sideways onto the cold stone. Utterly exhausted, he fell into a nightmarish sleep.

When Davy awoke he had difficulty for a moment in remembering where he was, and then, as he remembered and tried to straighten his limbs, he was gripped by an excruciating cramp. As he watched the thin light grow stronger, his mind turned to John Willie and Mr. Cartwright. How were they? What were they thinking? That he was dead, surely, that's what they would be thinking. And although Mr. Cartwright was a brave man, as all pitmen were, he was an old man. Sixty-four he was supposed to be, but it was known among the men that his real age was at least seventy. He kept on working because he wanted to keep a roof over the heads of his old wife and himself, for once you were finished working in the pit you had no more claim on a pit cottage, not unless you had a son working there also, and Mr. Cartwright had no children at all.

He stumbled to his feet and tried to stamp the circulation back into his legs. Then he began to call again. His voice throaty and hoarse, he repeated the words "Hie there! Help! Hie there!" until he felt utterly worn out.

When the light was shining more strongly down the shaft, he looked about him and noticed what he hadn't noticed last night, that there was a road at the far side of this junction. It was directly opposite to the one by which he had made his way here last night. Now why, he asked himself, had they made that passage if it didn't lead somewhere? And if, like the one he had come by, it sloped upward—well, who knew? He could but go up it and find out.

He looked up the shaft again, shouted once more, waited, listened, then turned about and stumbled across the roadway to the dark passage.

Here again he went onto his hands and knees and cautiously felt every inch of the road before moving forward. Yet he hadn't been crawling for more than ten minutes at the most when he sat back on his heels, and, his mouth open, his eyes stretched, he gazed ahead of him. He wasn't seeing things, was he? Perhaps it was another bore hole. But no, it was a different kind of light, sharper, different, *different!*

He was on his feet, stumbling forward, his hands now clutching at rough props, and when he suddenly pitched forward and fell across an iron rail he cried aloud, not with the pain of his fall but with joy. He was on a rolley way. He could see the road going off at an angle. This was where the horses used to pull the barrows full of corves. *He was on an old rolley way, he was on a rolley way. He was free.*

He picked himself up and ran now, uphill, uphill, uphill. And then he was in the open, standing on the hillside at the mouth of an old opencast mine.

He raised his eyes to the sky. He had never seen it so beautiful before; it was high and blue and warm. He was out in the world, he was alive, he was alive. He started to laugh while he knew he was crying. He wiped his hand hastily across the lower part of his face, then looked about him. There, not a hundred yards away, was the wall that surrounded the east side of Miss Peamarsh's property. He had come up out of the old disused opencast mine he knew so well; he was within a mile of the village and less than that from the pit cottages and his own home. And here all about him was the open fell land—open, that is, if you didn't count the pitheads. He must get to the pithead. He must take them back in there and get their John Willie and Mr. Cartwright out.

Stumbling and falling like a drunken man, he ran through heather clumps and over bare scree land, skirted Farmer Millbanks's field of barley—he daren't run through that, not for the life of him, although it would have cut short the distance. He ran and he ran until he came to the pit yard and collapsed at the feet of an astonished group of men.

Two

They had called him a clever young lad, a brave young lad, for hadn't he persevered where another might have given up, and thereby saved three lives? Well, two; two you could say; two that were of any use, for there were some bereaved women in the village who asked why God had spared a daft mute but had taken their men who were their means of livelihood and of keeping roofs over their heads, for now that their men were dead they would have no claim to their cottages. God's ways were indeed strange, past understanding.

Nor did the parson help their understanding when he appealed to them to submit to the will of God after he had buried the mass of bodies dragged up from the flooded mine. What did God know about empty bellies, and sleeping on the open fells, of young children dying from lack of food? God was for the rich mine owners, that's who God was for.

20

And so thought Davy as he ladled out the last spoonful of skilly onto John Willie's plate. He stood staring unseeingly down at the pan in his hand until a thin whine coming to him from the animal by his side brought his eyes to it, and with a sigh he spooned a dollup of the porridge up from his own plate and put it back into the pan, which he then pushed under the table for the dog.

When he sat down he did not attack his food, although he felt hungry. His belly had not felt full for over a week now. When he took a mouthful of the porridge it stuck in his throat, and he was unable to swallow, for John Willie's eyes were on him, and he saw that they were deep with understanding, and sadness—and fear. Oh yes, John Willie was frightened. Although he couldn't hear a word of what had been said along the road or in the village these past weeks, his eyes had read the signs, and he hadn't to be told that the situation was desperate, nor had he to be told that he was a handicap. He could sense things, could John Willie.

Davy lowered his gaze to his plate as he thought guiltily, I could get by on me own. If only I could put him someplace just for a while until I got settled, and then pick him up again. But there's one thing certain. If I have to go on the road, I can't take him with me. The autumn's almost on us and that'll be bad enough, but the winter'll kill him, if it doesn't me. . . . And we've got to be out of here by Saturday.

He now scraped up the remainder of his porridge from his plate and thrust it into his mouth as he thought angrily, 'Tisn't fair, 'tisn't fair; they should have set us on someplace else. It isn't as if there were all that many left. They could have done something for us. Then, his reason coming to his aid, he asked himself quietly, What could they have done, seeing that all the pits roundabout were manned to the full, and grown men just waiting to step into dead men's shoes, and not only in the pits, but in all types of jobs?

When he heard they had started a new shipyard in Jarrow trying out iron boats, he had walked the six miles there, only to be told no, they had all the labor they wanted. "Come back when you're grown up, lad," one gaffer had jeered at him, and he had thought, if I was grown up I'd punch you right in the teeth, I would that, while at the same time thinking how wonderful it would have been working above ground and in the daylight.

And then there was yet another problem. This was brought to his mind when John Willie slid from the chair and, walking slowly to the mat in front of the fire, sat down on it and put his arms around the dog who was lying there, then buried his face in its thick fur. What was going to become of Snuffy? He'd have to be put down. . . . Oh no!

The rejection of the idea brought him up from the table, and he gathered the plates together and the pan from the floor. Then, going to a table standing against the far wall on which there was a tin bowl of water, he washed the plates and spoons, and afterward put in the soot-coated pan and washed that.

This done, he carried the dish out of the back door and walked a few feet across the dried uneven mud of the yard, then threw the soot-covered water onto a fly-strewn refuse heap, one of a line that fenced the back of the cottages and the outside lavatories. He was returning to the house when he looked down the row and saw at the far end a group of the Coxon children squabbling as usual. Matthew Coxon, their father, had been the only householder in the row to survive the disaster, and he and two of his elder boys had been kept on at the pit to assist the overseer in the maintenance and pumping operations.

It would be a Coxon who would come out lucky.

Davy went in and banged the door; then he stood with his back to it for a moment, his eyes tightly screwed up, before thrusting himself away from its support. After putting the dish on the table, he roused John Willie and motioned to him that they were going out, and the intention of their walk he made evident by handing him a tin mug and himself taking up a straw basket. But even as he did so he knew that they couldn't live on berries and that he must do today what he had put off for the last week; he must go to Parson Murray's and ask him for a slip to take to the workhouse which would enable them to get bread, after they had paid for it, of course, by breaking up stones.

Before leaving the house he locked both doors. There wasn't much to steal, but that Coxon lot would be through it like a swarm of locusts if they could get in, especially knowing that he was on the road and would only be able to carry bedding and a pot or two. When other people were turned out of their homes they always managed to sell their bits and pieces to neighbors if only in exchange for food, or an extra blanket, but there was nobody left in the row to sell anything to, and those left in the village were hard put to it to find food. They wouldn't be able to buy anything from him, certainly not the new clippie mat which was the last thing his mother had made before she died two years ago and which as yet had never been put on the floor, nor even the jug.

His father had always talked about the jug as if it were made of gold instead of china. It was nigh on a hundred years old, he had said, and belonged to his great-grandmother. It had been given to her by her mistress on the day she married. They had lived far away in London town at the time, and her mistress's family were the makers of china. There was an animal on the jug, a sheep or a goat or something like that, and on the bottom there was a kind of ring with a triangle inside of it and some writing, but as no one in the family could read, they had never found out what the word was. But nevertheless the jug was held to be of some value, so much so that although it was a milk jug, it had never seen milk but had reposed on the mantelpiece as long as he could remember.

Well, he could take the jug with him, and if the worse came to the worst he could walk to Shields's Saturday market and sell it there, perhaps for as much as five shillings. His dad had always said it was worth a week's wages.

When John Willie tripped in a pothole on the rough road, he put out his hand quickly to save him, and his mind was brought back to the present and the purpose of their journey. The bushes on the fells were stripped bare, but inside the grounds of Gorge Manor fruit and berries were going rotten on the ground, and he knew that he must risk being discovered again by Miss Peamarsh, because they must eat.

He was aware that there would be very little fruit left on the ground, or on the bushes for that matter, if any of the Coxon children had discovered the hole in the wall, but it was well hidden by the six-foot hedge of bramble that ran along the entire length of the northern boundary. He would never have found it if one Sunday last winter, while risking being scratched and torn by brambles, he had not wriggled through the undergrowth in pursuit of a fleeing rabbit, hoping to come across its burrow. They'd had no meat in the house for weeks, and he was willing to endure torn hands and face for a fresh rabbit stew. It was then he had come up against the crumbling wall; the mortar had loosened between the bricks, and some had fallen away, leaving a gap of eighteen inches or more.

They were now passing the gates of the Manor, and he glanced up the long drive to where he could see the corner of the house in the distance. That's all he had ever seen of the house, but his mother had talked so much about it that he felt that if he were to see it he'd recognize it. It wasn't big as manor houses went, she had said, having only ten rooms, but it had been in the Peamarsh family for generations, and there'd always been a minister by the name of Peamarsh in this district until Parson Peamarsh died some eight years ago and Parson Murray took his place. Everybody had thought young Mr. George Peamarsh would follow in his father's footsteps and go into the ministry, but young Mr. George had been a wild 'un and had up and gone to foreign parts. And this had broken his father's heart, so much so that he'd had a stroke and had never spoken again from that day until the day he died two years later.

It was from that day, his mother said, that Miss Eleanor had gone funny, locking the place up, even going as far as not having a servant in the house after Dan and Mary Potter left.

Dan Potter had been gardening at the Manor from the time Parson Peamarsh had taken him, as a young boy, from the workhouse, and the village folk said he had forgotten all about the good that had been done to him when he came into the money from a relative in America. His good fortune had happened just after the old parson died, and he had up and left Miss Peamarsh on her own, and Mary, who had also worked in the house since she was a young girl and had married Dan Potter from there, went along with him, and what did they do but set up a grocery shop in Shields. And folks said they were making a pot of money.

But again, as folks said, give Dan his due, he did visit Miss Eleanor three or four times a year to see how she was getting on. He drove up in his covered van which was drawn by a fine gray horse, and there was always a fight among the lads to be the one to hold the horse while he went in to see Miss Peamarsh, because Miss Peamarsh, being funny like, wouldn't open the gates to let him drive through. And so he always lugged a basket of groceries up to the house himself; and when he came out he gave a penny to the one who was holding the horse's reins. It was usually one of the Coxons, the biggest one, because he could fight off the rest.

His mother had said that Miss Peamarsh had been a bonny lass when she was young and full of life. Well, Davy thought, he could imagine her being full of life, because she bawled loud enough now, but never bonny. She was so skinny she looked like a scarecrow.

He almost choked at this point in his thinking, for it was as if his thoughts had conjured the owner of the Manor up out of the ground . . . there she was standing before him. He had almost bumped into her as he turned the corner of the wall. He stepped back, pulling John Willie with him, and stared up at the tall figure glaring down on him, and all he could think to himself at the moment was, Oh lor! what now?

Miss Peamarsh had all the appearance of a female tramp, for her black cloak had a green sheen on it; her skirt looked as old as the cloak, and the mud-fringe round the bottom was worn in places up to the hem;

her boots too were not those favored by the gentry; but most curious of all, and what stamped her as an oddity, was that she wore no head covering. Ladies always wore hats, and women wore shawls, and female tramps wore sacks placed on their heads to look like pointed caps to serve the dual purpose of keeping both their heads and their backs dry. But Miss Peamarsh went about bareheaded, and any stranger could have been forgiven for not treating her as a lady. That is until she opened her mouth, and then everybody knew she was a lady, even if an odd one.

"Well! You again?"

Davy did not take his eyes from the grim visage, and his voice held an apologetic note as he said, "Aye, miss."

"What are you after now?"

"Just . . . just gatherin' berries, miss."

"Looking for a way to get into my grounds, I suppose. . . . Tell me, how did you get in before?"

He blinked, swallowed, then said, "I . . . I climbed the wall, miss."

"Climbed the wall!" She gave a disdainful jerk to her chin. "Don't lie to me. *You* might have climbed the wall, but *he* couldn't; he's too puny." She thrust a finger down at John Willie. "That wall is all of seven feet. And where could you climb it along here? It is covered with brush."

As she cast her glance back along the wall Davy knew that she had been examining it to find out how exactly he had got into the grounds. Then she surprised him completely by saying, "Your father died in a disaster and you got the others out, I hear."

He made no answer for a moment. How did she know that? It was said she never spoke to anybody in the village or hereabouts. But of course she would have known there was an accident, for she would have heard the disaster buzzer. He said now, "Aye, miss, but it was just luck and . . . and God's will."

"God's will!" There was another disdainful lift to her chin. "Don't talk like an old man, boy. What do you know about God's will?"

Aye, what did he know about God's will, except what Parson Murray told him?

She was now staring down at John Willie as she had done on the other two occasions when they had met, and John Willie was staring back at her.

Davy looked at his brother's face. He couldn't understand the expression on it. He was looking at Miss Peamarsh as if he liked her. It was the same look as he kept for Snuffy. Well, he could understand his feelings for Snuffy, but not for this woman. And it surely wasn't that he could think her nice in any way, for although he couldn't hear the tones of her voice, he could see the expression on her face, and, as on the other occasions, it was now anything but pleasant; her look was almost ferocious. Yet John Willie was looking softly at her.

"He looks like a seal."

"What!" he rapped out. Their John Willie looking like a seal? She was being nasty. He didn't mind her going for him, but she wasn't going to liken their John Willie to a fish, because that was what a seal was. He had never seen one, but he had heard tell of them, swimming round the islands off the coast. And their John Willie was no fish.

It was odd, but he rarely lost his temper on his own account, yet was quick to lose it on his brother's. And so now, in a tone that matched her own, he said, "He's no fish! He doesn't look like a fish."

"Who's talking about fish, boy?" She was looking

directly at him now. "I said he looked like a seal; he has the eyes of a seal."

"Oh!" He looked at his brother's eyes. He had nice eyes. They were big and soft-looking. He dared to smile now as he said, "Seals must have nice eyes then, miss."

"Haven't you ever seen a seal?"

"No, miss."

"Nor a picture of one?"

"No, miss. I . . . I can't read."

"Don't be stupid, boy. You don't have to read to understand a picture."

He gulped again. Oh, he'd like to say something to her, give her a mouthful. Stupid, was he?

"The pit is closed; where are you working?"

"Nowhere, miss." His voice was sullen now.

"How are you living, then?"

He was about to reply, "I don't know," when he realized that she would consider that a stupid answer and so he said, "I'm . . . I'm going on the road to look for work."

"That child will never stand the road; he looks too sickly." Again her finger was stabbing toward John Willie.

The spittle gathered in his throat and he had to swallow twice before he could say, "I'm . . . I'm going to the parson for a slip for bread, and . . . and when I'm at the workhouse I'm going to see if I can leave him there till . . . till I'm settled."

"The workhouse?"

"Yes, miss."

"Stupid . . . stupid, I say; he'll never survive there. Far better take him with you." She again stared down on John Willie.

And now John Willie spoke. "Huh!" he said.

"What is he saying?"

"I . . . I don't know."

"It must mean something—that, that sound."

"Aye. Aye, it usually does, but . . . but this time I don't know."

"Stupid boy! You should know. Sounds always mean something." With this parting shot she covered him with a final disdainful glance, then marched off.

Davy stood watching her walk away while his teeth ground against each other. She had called him stupid again. By lad! he would like to show her. He turned to his brother and was about to say, "Come on," but stopped as he saw him staring after the tall, shabbily dressed woman. John Willie was smiling, and now he looked up into Davy's face and again he said, "Huh!" And now Davy could interpret the word, and with a jerk of his head he barked, "Nice! You can have her. Nice! Don't be daft. Come on."

One thing was sure now, they couldn't go into the grounds, not today anyhow, with her on the warpath, and so, hiding the basket and mug in a clump of bushes, he made straight for the vicarage.

Parson Murray was a middle-aged man with a large family, a wide parish and a small stipend. He was also a kindly man. "I'm sorry for you, Davy," he said. "Your brother is going to need attention all his life, and I think you're wise in placing him in care until you're settled in some secure employment. If I could do anything to help you I would. . . . But there are so many destitute."

His voice trailed away, and Davy said, "It's . . . it's all right, sir, as long as you give me a ticket."

"Oh, I'll give you a ticket, Davy. But you know what will happen: they'll expect you to work for it."

"I know that, sir."

"It's very hard work, Davy."

Davy now made a sound very similar to that of John Willie's huh as he said, "I'm used to hard work, sir; I was bred on it."

"Of course, of course." The minister nodded his head. Then pointing to a wooden form in the hallway he said, "Sit down there while I write it out."

And so they sat looking round the sparsely furnished hall of the vicarage, and Davy listened to the clatter of pans and the sound of voices coming from the kitchen, and particularly the high tones of Mrs. Murray, and as Davy listened it seemed as if the parson's wife were instructing her daughters in some culinary art. "Two ounces is enough," she was saying; "use more flour."

Flour meant bread, but the parson's wife had never been known to give a crumb away. Well, he supposed, he couldn't blame her, not with eight daughters, the eldest only fifteen. There were two sons, but they were mere babies. God, he felt, was no respecter of parsons either, or else He would have put the boys at the other end.

Parson Murray came into the hall again, and after handing Davy a narrow slip of not too clean paper he bent his short back and pushed a ha'penny into Davy's hand, then did the same to John Willie.

"Oh . . . oh, thank you, sir. Thank . . ."

Before Davy could get any further the parson held a warning finger to his lips and, placing his hand on Davy's shoulder, almost hustled him to the door. And there he said, "Good luck, boy. And God go with you."

"Thank you, sir. Thanks for everything."

He now took John Willie's hand and hurried him down the rough path and out of the vicarage gates, and there he turned and smiled down on his brother, and they both opened their palms and looked at the small coins. A ha'penny. What was a ha'penny? You couldn't get much with a ha'penny. Yet at this moment it seemed a large amount because the parson had given it to them; the parson who himself was known to be as poor as a church mouse had given them a ha'penny each. He actually laughed now as he thought of what might have happened if Mrs. Murray had discovered her husband's generosity. Why, it would have made her jump out of her petticoat.

There were good people in the world, kind people in the world; they weren't all like Miss Peamarsh.

"Come on." He tugged John Willie into step with him, and it was only when, half an hour later, he came within sight of the workhouse walls that he stopped, and the effect of what he was about to do overwhelmed him.

Slowly he bent down, and now in elaborate sign language he explained. Pointing first to the formidable gray buildings, he then pushed his finger into the young boy's chest, after which he placed the flat of his hand on his own breast, bowed his head, then rose to his feet and did a standing march.

John Willie understood; he understood only too well. His eyes screwed up, his mouth opened wide, and from it was tumbled a rapid succession of huh's that grew louder in protest.

"Look! Look!" Davy rose to his feet and, taking John Willie by the shoulders, shook him as he cried, "Listen. Listen." He always said listen, even while he knew it was a silly thing to say.

John Willie now became quiet, still. His mouth closed, his eyes stretched wide; there was no movement in any part of his thin body while he stared into Davy's troubled face.

"I've got to go to . . . to find work." Davy now demonstrated digging with a shovel. After this he pointed in the direction opposite to the workhouse; then counting on his fingers, "One, two, three, four, five"—for that was one thing he could do; he could count up to twenty—he brought his arm in a wide circling movement, finishing up by once more placing his finger on John Willie's chest. And although John Willie made no sign whatever, Davy knew that his brother was aware of what lay in front of him.

Slowly now they went toward the gates. When he rattled the chain a man came out of the lodge and, looking through the bars, said, "Aye, what you after?"

"I've got a ticket for bread."

"Another one of 'em!"

The porter took a key that was hanging from his belt and unlocked the chain and pulled open the gates, and they went inside, John Willie walking so close to Davy's side that he almost impeded his movements.

"Go along there to the clerk; he'll see to you." The man pointed into the distance, and they went toward a door, then through it and into a bare flagstoned corridor. There were windows on one side of the corridor, and through them he looked onto a big yard that was walled on all sides by high buildings. The yard was full of people, men, women, and children, and they were all doing odd things. Some were standing with their faces to the wall, some were jumping up and down as if skipping but without ropes; others were laughing. But there was one woman near the window almost within arm's length of him who had her face turned up to the sky, and the tears were washing her cheeks. Then there was the noise. It was a chattering noise, a mixture of all kinds of noises like those made by birds in a cage.

"They're the dafties."

He swung round startled to look up at a big, gangling woman who had a wooden bucket in one hand and a scrubbing brush and dirty cloth in the other, and she nodded her head toward the window as she grinned widely, saying, "They're all daft, barmy. I'm not daft. I'm Emma Steel, and I'm not daft." At this she turned and walked away to the end of the corridor, where, putting the bucket on the ground, she knelt down by it and started to scrub the stones.

It was some seconds before Davy realized that he was still staring at her, his mouth slightly agape. She'd said she wasn't daft. Well, she wasn't among that lot, but he had never seen anybody look dafter.

"What do you want?"

He swung round in the other direction now and looked at a woman in a kind of uniform dress with a starched cap on her head. The woman scrubbing the corridor had a cap on her head too, but it was a different one; and all those women out in the yard, they were wearing caps, like bonnets, dirty white bonnets.

"I've got a ticket"—he held out the slip—"for bread from . . . from Parson Murray."

"Go in the end door."

"Ta." He nodded at the woman as she walked away, and it was some seconds still before he could make his feet move toward the door at the end of the corridor.

When he opened the door he found he was looking into a room where four men were seated at high desks, and all were writing rapidly. The one nearest the door lifted his head and stared from Davy to John Willie, then back to Davy before saying, "Aye, what is it?"

Davy repeated that he had a ticket for bread and held it out. The man looked at the slip of paper. Then, raising his head and looking from one to the other again, he said, "For the two of you?"

"Yes, sir."

"You'll have to do four hours stone breaking, you know."

"Yes, sir."

"I can't see him breaking many stones."

"I . . . I can do enough for us both."

"No, no, it doesn't work like that; a man can only work to his full capacity, as can a boy. You are expected to give full capacity in return for your food."

"I'll work extra hard, sir."

The man was again looking at John Willie. "What is the matter with him? He's puny. How old is he?"

"Ten, sir. He's . . . he's deaf and dumb, sir."

"Deaf and dumb? Ten?" The man gave a little shake with his head as if he didn't believe it, then added not unkindly, "If you work all day you can have a midday meal."

"If . . . if you don't mind, sir, I'll . . . I'll just take the bread."

There was rising in Davy a desperate urge to be away from this place.

The man now took a metal disc from a drawer and, handing it to Davy, said, "I'm only giving you one 'cos he'll be no good at it. Go to the yard. See Mr. Rider, the officer; he'll show you to the road where they're breaking."

Davy looked down at the disc. There was an anger rising in him against the injustice of not giving John Willie a disc that would enable him to have his share of bread. Before he should give vent to it, however, he turned sharply away, dragging John Willie with him.

Out in the corridor again, he walked back to the woman who was scrubbing the floor. "Where's the yard?" he asked her.

"Yard? Through there, you daftie." She pointed to another corridor going off the main one.

Quickly he turned from her and went down the corridor that led to the yard. This yard, too, he saw was full. Women of all ages were shoveling coal into buckets while others carried the buckets away. At one side of the yard under a wooden awning women were bent over poss tubs, wielding the heavy poss sticks up and down, up and down, on the wet clothes. There were great mounds of moleskin trousers and gray twill dresses near every tub.

He passed by a low building from where the smell of hot irons issued. Some of the women looked up at them; others looked too lost in despair. These latter were generally those who had small children around them. When he asked where he could find Mr. Rider, he was directed to a short fat man who was hustling two small boys who were attempting to push a barrow of broken stone over the rough uneven flags of the yard.

"Bread. Four hours?" The man's small eyes scrutinized Davy. "Only four hours and only one of you?" he said; then, looking down on John Willie, he added, "He can help push the barrows."

"No, no, he can't; he's not goin' to. He's not earnin'. The man back there said he's not earnin', so he'll stay with me."

"Be careful, young 'un, be careful, else you'll get me fist in yer mouth and me toe in yer backside, an' that'll be in place of bread."

"Just try it on." Davy was past caution now; all he wanted was to get out of this place. He had heard about the workhouse—he had heard terrible things about the workhouse; he had seen the poor apprentices from the workhouse in the pit; they were always given the worst jobs and received the worst treatment.

The man glared at him, and Davy glared back.

Then from between his teeth he said, "You young scut, you! Get goin'," and he pointed in the direction of an opening in the yard.

But Davy took his time in going; he outstared the man for some seconds before turning away. And then he made his step slow and steady, which was difficult, as John Willie was pressing so closely against him.

When Davy left the yard he saw the men and the stones; they were making a kind of road leading across some farmland.

The man in charge of the work took the wind out of Davy's aggressive sails by saying, "Four hours, is it, lad? Aw well, just carry on in that corner. He hasn't got a disc, the young 'un?"

"No."

"Well no, I don't suppose they'd give him one. Anyway, just carry on over there next to that big fellow. All right?"

Davy nodded, then went toward the tall man. He was redheaded and looked in his mid-thirties.

"What do I do?"

The man stopped his rhythmic hammering of a chisel into a block of stone. "Same as me. Take the pick of your tools." He nodded toward the edge of the road. "And don't hurry or else you won't last."

And that's all the man said for the next hour.

But his silence did not affect Davy, who was too full of his own thoughts. Every now and again he would look in the direction of John Willie where he sat by the heap of broken stones, his head bent, his back bowed, his whole attitude showing his dejection, and he wanted to explain to him that it was all right; for if it meant their starving he had no intention of leaving him in this mad hole. But he couldn't explain without attracting the notice of the other men at work and pointing out to everybody that his brother was a deaf-mute.

When the man did speak it was about John Willie. "What's the matter with him?" he asked. "Is he sick?"

"No, not really; he's deaf and dumb."

"Poor devil."

"Are . . . are you in for good?"

"In for good?" The rhythmic hammering stopped and the red head went back and the man laughed aloud before he answered, "Not me, son, not me. It was only that me tongue hadn't licked food for three days that brought me in here."

"Are you from these parts?"

"Near enough; Durham."

"Oh, Durham. In the pits?"

"Aye, in the pits, or was."

"Everybody's out these days."

"Oh, it wasn't a case of being out; plenty of work in my pit."

Now Davy gave the man his full attention. "Then . . . then why are you here?"

"They got rid of me. Ever hear of unions?"

"Aye; aye, I've heard of unions."

"Well, if you get started in the pit in future, lad, and you want to keep your job, don't agitate for unions. That's my advice."

"They put you out for that?"

"Aye, they put me out for that. I'm on the blacklist. But not for long; no, not for long." He changed his rhythm and hammered three successive quick blows on the chisel. "Come the day when we'll be on top.

Do you know that, lad? We the pitmen'll be on top—
not all the bosses, or gods'll get the better of me."
Davy said nothing to this. He knew that the man
wasn't referring to working at the pithead but to getting one over on the bosses, and if there was ever
wishful thinking, that was wishful thinking, imagining
you could get one over on the bosses. But it was a
wonderful idea, although it would never come to anything. His mother had always said, "There'll always be
bosses and there'll always be workmen," and he be-
lieved she was right. However could a man be paid for
his work if there weren't men with money to pay him?
Yes, there'd always be bosses. He wished at this moment he was working for a boss, any boss, but prefera-
bly one who gave him orders above ground in the
daylight. Aye, it would be wonderful to be able to earn
his living in daylight, even in a job such as he was
doing now. But not in here. Oh no! not in here.

Time went on; then a whistle blew and the man in
charge shouted, "Time for grub!"

The red-haired man laid down his tools and said,
"Well, stop that and come on."

Davy stopped his hammering, and looking up at his
companion he said, "I'm just workin' for the bread—
four hours."

"Oh, I'm sorry. Be seeing you then."

"Aye, be seein' you."

But Davy didn't see the man again, for when those
who had eaten returned there were whispering and
laughing along the road, and without being told Davy
knew what had happened. The man had done a bunk;
he'd had his meal and done a bunk. He'd heard of
workhouse boys doing a bunk, but they were nearly
always caught and brought back and lathered.

Under other circumstances Davy would have

laughed aloud, but all he said to himself was, "He might have been starving, but he must have had some strength left to climb over that wall," because it was higher than the one surrounding Miss Peamarsh's grounds, and it had broken glass bottles along its top.

It was an hour later when Davy left the road, and he almost had to drag John Willie with him: the boy was so dejected. At one point Davy put his doubled fist under John Willie's chin in an effort to raise his head and tell him it was all right. But John Willie still kept his chin tucked into his chest.

The man who was doling out the bread had a quirk to his lips as he said, "One disc, one loaf," then thrusting his hand to the back of a shelf he brought out a small loaf and banged it onto the wooden table. Davy picked it up without looking at it, for he was returning the man's stare.

The loaf held in the crook of his arm and tugging John Willie with him, he threaded his way among the milling inmates across the yard to the corridor, where in vain he tried to keep his eyes from the windows and the mad specimens cavorting in the yard beyond. Then he was walking toward the iron gates, and as he went he felt the tension running from his brother's hand, and without looking at him he knew that his head was up and his face alight.

Not until they had passed through the gates and the feeling of freedom was on him once more did Davy look down on John Willie, and then that tenderness that would assail him at times came over him now, and it was all he could do to stop his own tears from flowing, for his brother's face was awash. But when the boy threw himself at him and his thin arms gripped his thigh, the lump in his throat threatened to choke him, and, shaking himself free from John Willie's hold, he gabbled down at him, "Stop it now! Stop it. You're all right. You understand? You're all right. Never, never." He jerked his thumb over his shoulder toward the gates, then repeated, "Never, never." After which he thrust his forefinger into John Willie's chest and then into his own and then crossed his fingers, and John Willie, gazing up at him almost with a look of adoration, nodded his head and smiled. And Davy smiled back at him.

Now since they were both so hungry he started to break an end off the loaf, but his fingers became still on the crust. The smile slid from his face; the loaf was hard, stale. He remembered the man stretching into the back of the shelf. He likely kept a number of such there as the means of venting his spite. Eeh! some people were awful, awful. He tore and twisted at the end of the loaf until he managed to break off a piece. This he broke in two and handed one piece to John Willie. Then they walked slowly back along the road home. Home that would only be theirs for another two days.

It was when he came to the wall surrounding Miss Peamarsh's property that the feeling of defiance swept over him.

He stood glaring at the bramble-strewn wall, the basket he had just retrieved gripped tightly in his hand. Over there was food of a sort; out here there was nothing. He now grabbed hold of John Willie's hand and, pulling him toward the concealed opening, pushed him downward onto the ground, then thrust him forward and followed him. But when they reached the hole, he grabbed John Willie's shoulder and stopped him from going through, and in the dim light that filtered through the tangled branches he indicated to him that he stay put and wait for him. Then, wriggling on his hands and knees, he went over the broken masonry and into the grounds.

The tangle was almost as thick this side of the wall as it was on the outside, for there was bramble growing among old currant bushes. As he crawled farther forward the orchard took over, and tangle thinned out into tall grass that was now dying into hay.

This is where he had come the first time. Then he had seen that the trees were full of fruit, but not quite ripe. Now they were almost bare except in the high top branches. But there were plenty of bruised apples and pears buried in the grass. He knew that to the left of him was the field where the cow was, but he daren't risk another attempt to milk her, not today at any rate, for he was too weary, too despondent. All he hoped for today was a hotchpotch of apples, pears and berries that he could stew together, and with the bread, such as it was, it would make a meal of sorts.

He rose to his feet, but with his back still bent he began to scramble through the long grass in search of the fruit. Some of the apples he picked up were so rotten that his fingers went through them. There were none without wasp holes. But what did that matter?

The basket was almost full when he happened to glance upward, and he caught his breath and almost choked on the sight of the tall thin figure of Miss Peamarsh coming, so he imagined, straight toward him. But when she stopped and looked to the side, then reached up into the branches of a tree, he dropped like a stone into the grass, where he lay hardly breathing until he realized that if she came straight on she would likely step on him.

Slowly now he began to wriggle like a snake through the long grass. There was a slight breeze blowing, so he reasoned that she would not be attracted by any movement he made. At one point he had turned his body round in what he imagined was the direction toward the wall, but after a few minutes when he found himself still crawling through the long grass he knew he wasn't going toward the wall, at least not where the hole lay.

He stopped his crawling and listened. There was no sound of footsteps. Slowly he raised his head above the grass, and to his amazement he saw that his crawling had brought him almost to the border of an open space. This, too, was grassy and must have been at one time a big fine lawn, but he saw it was now kept comparatively well cropped by four geese. He didn't know she kept geese. And it was funny he hadn't heard them squawking either. Then part of the reason for this was explained when he saw that this field, or lawn, almost faced the back of the house and was quite a distance from the road.

He stared at the house. It had a lonely look. Then again he saw Miss Peamarsh, but this time he didn't duck, for she had her back to him as she walked toward the house.

When she disappeared inside the house he crawled no more, but, rising slowly, he turned about and started to walk through the grass to where he had been gathering the apples. But he hadn't taken more than a dozen steps when he stopped. There in front of him, about six yards from where he stood, was an old summerhouse. It was almost hidden by the undergrowth, and it was evident that no one had been near it for some time, for the grass was growing up straight through the wooden boards of the steps and also of the little verandah.

He stood at the bottom of the steps and looked up at the door, which was hanging at a slant. Then his eyes flicked to the little windows on each side of the door. He was about to go up the steps when he stopped himself. Then his head jerked upward as if lifted by a bright idea.

Now he ran to the side of the summerhouse. But there his chin dropped somewhat and his head came down to its usual level when, having skirted the little place, he saw that the only windows were in the front, and even from where he stood he could see that they were fixed tight with age.

It looked as if the only access to the deserted place were through that broken door. But once he had removed that and trampled the grass down on the steps and verandah in the process of getting in, who was to know she wouldn't come by at some time and notice?

It surprised him somewhat to find that he had already made up his mind that this was the place in which he was going to seek shelter. The only problem was how to get in.

The summerhouse, he noticed, was made of weatherboarding, one slat overlapping the other. Well now, he had only to start from the bottom and loosen two or three and he'd have a way in. The back was half buried in a tangle of brambles, which was all the better. The only thing they would have to do was to be very quiet. But that would prove no problem: There could be no one more quiet than John Willie. . . . But . . . but what about Snuffy?

Yes, what about Snuffy? Well, he was obedient, wasn't he? He did what he was told. He was a sheep dog and had once been used for herding the sheep on the hills. His da had come across him limping along a field path and had seen that the beast was pretty near his end, having caught his back paw in a trap at some time. He had likely been turfed out when he was no longer of any use. He had given the dog a bit of his bait and the animal had followed him home. And that was how Snuffy had come into the family.

He remembered the very day the dog had limped into the house and the excitement that filled him at the first sight of the bedraggled collie, and when the beast came up to him and sniffed all round his face he had laughed and said, "He's snuffing me." And that's how he'd got his name.

His da had been very fond of Snuffy; in fact, on looking back, Davy knew that his father had been kinder to the animal than he had been to his younger son.

But the trouble about bringing Snuffy into the old summerhouse was that he might bark. He barked at rabbits and ran after them in his lopsided way, whereas if he saw sheep he would just stand and quiver.

Davy bowed his head and shook it slowly. Whatever plans he made for the future would have to include Snuffy, not only for his own sake but for John Willie's, because John Willie and Snuffy had become inseparable.

He now pushed his way through the bramble and tested the boards at the back of the summerhouse by inserting his fingers under the bottom board where it had shrunk away from the stone base, and when he pulled it he almost fell onto his back with the whole board in his hand. The next one and the next came away just as easily. And then, lying on his side, he was squeezing his way through.

Rising to his feet, he looked about him in the dimness. The place was very small; it looked smaller inside than it did from the outside. He guessed it was about eight feet long by six wide. There was a round bamboo table in one corner—the cane had split and was sticking out at all angles; in another corner was a similarly made chair, and on its seat was what had once been a cushion, but from the condition of it now he saw that it had made more than one nest for mice or small animals of some kind.

He stood nodding to himself. This would do. This would do fine. It was very evident that nobody had been in here for years. He'd bring their bedding in, but he'd have to cook outside the grounds on the fell somewhere.

They wouldn't, he decided, come in until nighttime when the dusk was deepening, and during the daytime he'd go round looking for work. He might get set on tatie picking, that is if he was out early enough, for they'd be lining up for tatie picking this year. And because of this the farmers would cut their rates, knowing they had the upper hand, with a dozen or more men for every job, even for such a mundane one as tatie picking. Nevertheless, he could but try.

But one thing he must be careful of, and that was that the Coxons didn't get wind of where they were sleeping. For when they saw him and John Willie still about the place, they would want to know where they were staying, so he would tell them in the old mine. And he'd go further: he'd leave the pans and a few odds and ends there in case the Coxons went in looking for them. And that was a thought: he could cook there. When it was raining he could build a fire at the entrance, and they'd be able to eat where it was dry.

At one time he had considered camping out in the mine, but John Willie had become very agitated when he took him in, so much so that he had been sick. It must have been the memory of the long dark night he had spent in there alone with Mr. Cartwright that had put the fear in him.

When a few minutes later he crawled back through the hole in the wall, John Willie grabbed his hands and opened his mouth on the point of uttering a relieved "Huh!" but quickly Davy cautioned him to silence. Then they crawled out to where the brushwood thinned, and then they rose to their feet and went into the open through the long grass and so emerged onto the road as if they had just been searching for berries in the thicket.

It would happen, thought Davy some five minutes later, that they would run into the Coxons, and here he was with the apples exposed in the basket, having nothing to cover them with.

Mr. Coxon and the two eldest boys, Arthur, who was Davy's age, and Fred, who was a year younger, came striding toward them, swinging full bait tins.

"Well, hie up there! What we got here, apples? Been scrumping?" Mr. Coxon thrust his hand forward into the basket and picked up an apple that was marred by only one or two wasp holes. "Nice lot there. Where did you get those, lad?"

"Back yonder."

"Back yonder! Listen to him." Fred Coxon, who, although smaller than either his brother Arthur or Davy himself, was the most aggressive of all the Coxons, repeated, "Back yonder! Could be Jarrow, Wallsend, or Newcastle. Back yonder! You're not goin' to say, are you?"

"Quiet, lad!" His father pushed him on the shoulder. "Davy doesn't mind tellin' us where he got the apples, though I know of no orchard within two miles of here."

Glaring at Fred Coxon, Davy now said, " 'Twas a place yon side Hebburn. I don't know the name of the farm."

"And if you did you wouldn't say."

"No, you're right; I wouldn't say."

As the two boys glared at each other Arthur Coxon said, "Aw, come away; he'll need all the apples he can get after Saturda'."

He pulled hard at his brother and they went to move on. But Mr. Coxon didn't join his sons. Looking at Davy, he said, "Aye, Saturda'. Have you thought what you're gonna do with your bits and pieces?"

"Sell them."

"You'll be lucky, lad. Who's gonna buy 'em?"

"I'll find somebody. One thing's sure: I'm not goin' to leave them there."

"No, lad, I can understand you wouldn't want the Irish to have them. And that's who's comin' in, the Irish."

"The Irish are comin' into the row?" Davy's eyes were wide.

"Aye, all but into my place, 'cos it looks as if there's gonna be trouble at the High Main pit. The overseers have got wind of it, so they're shippin' more Irish in ready to take over should the fools go on strike."

Davy stared at Mr. Coxon. Then he said quietly, "You wouldn't go on strike, Mr. Coxon, would you?"

Matthew Coxon's face darkened, his chin knobbled, his lower lip was thrust out and his head moved from side to side before he growled, "I've got a family to bring up, an' responsibilities. I'm a responsible man.

Let the hotheads do what they like. I mind me own business. And what I was leading up to, boy, was an act of kindness; I was gonna say we would look after your big stuff for you till you got a place. And I'll still say it; I'm a man of me word.''

It was on the tip of Davy's tongue to answer, "I'd rather see the Irish have our pieces," but what he said was, "Thanks all the same, but I've already made arrangements.''

"Aw, have you?"

"Aye, I have.''

On this Davy nodded his head once, and as he went to turn away Mr. Coxon threw the apple back into the basket with such force that it split in two, and he growled, "Well, good luck to you!" and his gaze falling on John Willie he ended, "An' you'll need it with that hump on yer back. We'll come and see you when you're in the workhouse for good; your visit was short yesterda'.''

Davy stood glaring at the undersized man as he stamped away and joined his sons. News sped on the wind, didn't it? You couldn't blink but somebody knew about it. Well, there was one thing sure, the Coxons wouldn't get his bits and pieces. He'd go in the morning and see Mr. Cartwright; he'd be only too glad of them, for they hadn't all that much furniture in their house, and he'd help push it there on a barrow, aye, even if it took half a dozen journeys. But if for some reason Mr. Cartwright didn't take the stuff, then he'd burn it. Aye, he would; he'd take it out on the fells and heap it up and burn it. His mother's good round table, the four wooden chairs, the rocking chair, the delf rack and the blanket box, yes, even the boards from the wooden bed, he'd burn the lot rather than let that blackleg get his hands on them.

Three

By Saturday morning the cottage was stripped of all but what they could carry on their backs. Mr. Cartwright had taken the furniture with gratitude, and Davy had made a number of journeys through the wall to the old summerhouse in Miss Peamarsh's grounds, even going so far as to carry in the biscuit mattress that he and John Willie slept on.

The mattress had been the most troublesome, for he couldn't risk taking it until after dark, and it was one thing finding his way cautiously through the tangled grounds in the daytime but quite another at night lumbered with a mattress on his back.

It was in broad daylight on the Saturday morning that he closed the door behind him for the last time and they set off in full view of the Coxon family. The bulk of their clothing was strapped to his own back, together with two blankets, and across one shoulder was strung the kettle and two pans, and in his hand, wrapped in a knotted bait handkerchief, he carried the jug.

John Willie, too, seemed loaded down with baggage, for his small frame was almost obliterated by the blanket on his back. In one hand he carried a bundle, and in the other he held the piece of rope that was attached to a rope collar around Snuffy's neck.

"Hope you come across that orchard again, lad," Mr. Coxon sneered as Davy passed him. "You'll need all the bruised fruit you can get, now the nights are drawin' in."

The whole Coxon family seemed to have assembled to see them off, and the children laughed, and when one of them cried, "Donkeys go better laden," it was as much as he could do not to punch him.

The bitterness grew in him as he went down the road, and again he thought, People are awful, and your own kind are the worst.

Yet he reminded himself there were also people like Mr. Cartwright and his wife.

Mr. Cartwright had said last night that he'd had it in his mind to take them both into his house, until his wife had told him she had already hinted to Mrs. Joblin that she could have their other room.

Mrs. Joblin had lived in their row of cottages, three doors below them. Her man had been drowned in the disaster, and she had two wee children and another waiting to be born. And so he had told Mr. Cartwright that he understood Mrs. Joblin's need and he hadn't to be troubled about them; they'd get by.

Mrs. Cartwright had given them a whole oven-bottom cake. If they were sparing, it would last them three days, and if he could catch a rabbit they wouldn't do too badly at all.

Just in case one of the Coxons might follow them, he walked across the fell toward the disused mine, but when they came in sight of it John Willie stopped. His attitude like that of a balking horse, he stuck his heels in the ground, and Snuffy stopped with him.

Gazing down in irritation on his brother, Davy said harshly, "It's all right; we're not going in"; then he demonstrated with his hands that they were going back toward the wall. But still John Willie wouldn't be reassured. He voiced his distress with a succession of sounds.

Impatiently now Davy walked on, and after a while John Willie trailed slowly behind him. When, his head lowered, he came up to Davy waiting at the mouth of the opencast mine, Davy pressed him to the ground none too gently and, wagging his finger at him, said, "Stay." Then, looking at Snuffy, he repeated the command, "Stay!" but added, "you and all," and the dog immediately lowered himself to the ground; and, like John Willie, he looked up at Davy, and there seemed to be the same expression in his eyes as in those of the child by his side.

Davy had taken but a few strides forward when he stopped and, returning to John Willie, handed him the jug, patting it gently as he did so, which told his brother to be careful of it. Then he moved forward again down the long incline and into the mine.

But no sooner had he left the daylight than his own self-possession left him, for not only did he feel entirely alone in the whole wide world and afraid of the future, but equally he was afraid of the darkness into which he was walking; and he realized in this moment that if he were offered a job in a pit he'd find it difficult to go down below again.

He knew he could feel his way to the end of the rolley lines, but so strong was the feeling of fear on him that he decided that this was as far as he was going. And so, taking a pan and two old mugs from the sling, and a blanket from the bundle on his back, he placed them on a shelf of stone some distance above the road in such a way that anyone with a light such as one of the Coxons might have would pick them up immediately.

During the time he had worked down the pit he had never experienced this particular kind of fear. It stemmed, he thought, from the panic of the darkness, that seemingly eternal blackness through which they had crawled hour after hour. And only in this moment did he understand John Willie's feelings; for his brother, who was unable either to hear or to speak, the fear must have been threefold.

Almost at a stumbling run now he made for the light. John Willie was sitting exactly as he had left him, the dog also, and he smiled down on them as he said, "Come on, up with yous!" and, holding out his hand, he pulled his brother to his feet.

Before he could install them all safely in the summerhouse Davy had to do some preliminary work while it was still light. To begin with, he led both John Willie and Snuffy cautiously through the undergrowth and showed them what they had to do to get inside. It meant lying flat and edging sideways until one was clear of the boards.

It was an exercise even more necessary for the dog than it was for John Willie, but Snuffy quickly realized what was required of him. Stretching out his good back leg and his two front ones, he slithered after John Willie and entered his new home with interest. After sniffing around the corners of the little room, he turned his shaggy head up to Davy and, his mouth wide and his tongue lolling, seemed to say, "This is fine by me."

Then having led them back again through the undergrowth and so on to the fell land, Davy unearthed from a hidey-hole the extra utensils he had hidden there earlier on. He now built a fire in a hollow, and having brought a pan of water from a small brook that trickled down between the stones on its way to the river Tyne, he let the water boil before throwing into it the last masking of tea he had, afterward dividing it between the two mugs.

After they had drunk the scalding liquid, he gathered together the used tea leaves and placed them, with the remains of other brewings, in a discolored linen bag for further use, and only then did he share out an allotted portion of bread from the oven-bottom cake Mrs. Cartwright had given him, for he had found that if your belly was full of hot liquid you didn't crave so much solid food.

It was when John Willie went to give Snuffy half of his small piece of the bread that Davy checked him sharply, saying, "Eat it yourself; he can scrounge." But when he looked at the dog sitting patiently, while his eyes begged for some small offering, he snapped off a piece from his own portion and, thrusting it at Snuffy, said, "Aw there, get it down you."

When John Willie went to follow suit, however, Davy's hand came out roughly and struck at him, almost knocking him onto his back; but as quickly he righted him and mouthed at him, at the same time making signs, that he had to eat, and he finished, "For

God knows where the next'll come from after the morrow.''

John Willie stared up at his square-faced, tawnyheaded brother, the brother who had been father, mother and God to him, and would ever be so; and he slowly put out his hand, and with a gentle stroking movement his fingers caressed Davy's arm.

This forgiving gesture was almost too much for Davy. As always, it had the power to weaken him, and make him want to bubble his eyes out. He got sharply to his feet, then indicated that the light was going and they'd better be on their way.

Fifteen minutes later they were crawling through the hole in the wall, but this time John Willie went first, for even in the dim light he could remember the path. That was something he was good at, remembering. He had only to be shown how to do a thing once and he had it; but it had to be something that didn't require strength, for in this respect he was greatly lacking.

Davy, following him, held on to the rope around Snuffy's neck to make sure that no night animal would attract his attention and cause him to scurry away into the undergrowth.

When at last they were all safely inside the summerhouse it was too dark to see anything, but their bed was laid out to the side, away from the draught of the door, with the blankets already on it.

Drawing John Willie down onto the tick, he pulled off his clogs, then pushed him under the blankets, after which he took off his own clogs, pulled his sweatcaked stockings away from the soles of his feet and wriggled his toes. Then, having taken off his coat only, he too got into the bed. Lastly, he pulled Snuffy toward him and onto the foot of the bed; then he took one more precaution; he made a loop at the end of the rope attached to Snuffy's rude collar and slipped it over his wrist. Only then did he lie down, to drop almost immediately into a heavy, dream-filled sleep.

It was some ten hours later when Davy awoke, and he lay on his back staring upward for a full minute looking at the cobwebbed timbers in the roof and trying to recollect where he was. Slowly he moved his head to the side and met the wide smiling gaze of his brother, who was sitting patiently looking down on him, as was Snuffy, who was stretched to his full length up the bed.

Davy gave a little sound like a laugh and smiled at John Willie as he said, "Well, well. I slept, didn't I? An' we made it." He turned his head now and looked around the small space. The morning light showed up the dirt and decay as he hadn't seen it before. Long trails of ivy which had worked their way between the boards were hanging down like curtains right opposite him.

Slowly, he got up out of the bed and stretched, then took three short steps to the doorway. But when John Willie made to follow him he quickly signaled him to be still.

As he looked over the broken door his hand came up to his face and across his mouth. There she was, Miss Peamarsh. He could see her clearly, all except her feet. She had just come out of the back door; she had a basket on her arm, which indicated to him she was going to gather eggs.

He watched her stop, then heard her call to the geese, which were cackling away at this side of the clearing and not very far from the summerhouse itself.

When the geese didn't answer her bidding, he stood holding his breath for a moment in case she should come in this direction; then he reassured himself: even if she did, would she be likely to make her way to this place which she hadn't apparently bothered to enter for years? Nevertheless, as he watched her move away in the direction of the field where the cow was and the hens were scratching, he resolved that this was the last time he'd be here to watch her go on her morning rounds, for after this they'd be away as soon as light broke.

And so it was; every morning for the next fortnight they were outside the wall as dawn broke, and during that time it looked as if Davy's luck had turned, for although he didn't find work in the fields straightaway, twice he found a loaf and half the carcass of a cooked rabbit near the pan on the shelf in the mine. And one morning there was another blanket.

He knew that this was Mr. Cartwright's doing, for he had told him, too, that they would be sleeping in the mine, and the fact that he had left only one blanket there had caused the old man to add another to it. He was kind, was Mr. Cartwright, and Davy vowed that when he got a steady job he would pay him back. Indeed he would. He didn't look upon the old man's kindness as part payment for the oddments of furniture.

And then for three whole days he was taken on tatie picking, but just as extra labor; the farmer wanted the fields cleared while the weather was dry. And John Willie, too, was employed, at twopence a day for holding the sacks.

With three shillings and sixpence in his pocket he

and John Willie and Snuffy walked the three miles into Jarrow; and when they walked back their bellies were comparatively full, for he had spent threepence on three plates of pease pudding, and in the sack on his back he had a whole sheep's lights, a pound of chitterlings, two loaves of bread, two ounces of tea, a pound of streaky bacon, a half-pound of sugar and a pound of pig's fat. And after spending all that, he still had sixpence in his pocket, John Willie's sixpence as he thought of it.

He had been tempted to buy John Willie a pennorth of treacle taffy but had thought better of it, knowing it was an extravagance he might regret before many days were over their heads.

In the fields and on his journeying he had met a number of miners he had known, and they all promised that should they get set on they'd remember him. But such a promise, as his mother would have said, was like the saying, "Live, horse, and you'll get grass."

And as the days went on, he asked himself what he was going to do. There was no more chance of being set on in the fields. All the taties were up, and the swede turnips an' all. But still, as he said reassuringly to John Willie, something would turn up, he felt sure of it. . . . That was, until the rain started.

The first week in October had been sunny, even warm, but on the Monday of the second week the rain started in the night. It woke him when it spattered down on his face through the leaking slats of the roof. And he had to get up and pull their bed into another corner. He accomplished this without arousing John Willie, but not Snuffy, and when the dog got up and whined, he hissed at it, "That's enough. Shut up!"

The rain turned into a gale, and such was the force of it that they didn't go out all day. Except to take flying trips outside to do their business, the three of them sat huddled together on the mattress, cold and hungry, and all three miserable.

On the second morning the rain had not let up. They had eaten the last of their food early on the previous day, so there was no alternative if they wanted to get to the village but to face the storm.

They did not go to their own village because it did not have a shop but to a village which lay on the road to Jarrow. Here the village shop wasn't a tommy shop, in which the miners were often forced, through their bonds, to buy their groceries at exorbitant prices. But even so the owner of the shop charged high, and all they got for threepence was a loaf of bread and half an ounce of the cheapest tea.

He had visited the mine a number of times of late but had found nothing on the shelf. Either Mr. Cartwright was bad, he thought, or he was having to pull his own belt in. In case it might be the latter, he restrained the hungry desire to pay him a visit, for, as he thought of it, such a visit might put Mr. Cartwright on an awkward foot.

In case of an emergency like the present he had left dry kindling in the mouth of the mine, and after lighting a fire he eventually got the kettle to boil and brewed some tea. And this he divided into three, for he realized that Snuffy too was almost starving. After adding more boiling water to the tea leaves, he poured the liquid into the can and they set off once again through the rain for the summerhouse.

It was when they arrived at the summerhouse sodden to the skin and faint with hunger that John Willie began to cough, and when he kept on, Davy took him by the shoulders and shook him, then wagged his finger threateningly in his face, hissing, "Stop it! Stop it!" He patted his throat, shook his head, then pointed toward the door which had slipped farther down in the gale. Now turning from John Willie, he stared at the door for a moment before rushing at it, lifting it upright and so blocking the entrance with it.

Why hadn't he thought of that before? He'd keep the door upright at night, then put it back into its slanting position in the mornings.

He now stripped John Willie of all his clothes, took a rough piece of hessian that acted as a towel, and rubbed the small thin body all over with it until he could feel the warmth under his hands; then he put him into bed and covered him up. He now made him drink some of the still warm tea that was merely colored water. And he had almost finished the remainder himself when he felt Snuffy's eyes on him, and with an "Aw, you!" he poured the remaining liquid into a tin bowl and put it down before the dog.

Having taken his own clothes off, he was rubbing himself with the towel when Snuffy thought it was about time that he, too, should get rid of the surplus water clinging to him, and so he shook himself vigorously. When the spray hit Davy's bare body he jumped aside, lost his balance and fell on the bed, almost on top of John Willie. There he lay for a moment looking at Snuffy; then he turned his head slowly and gazed down on John Willie, whose face was just a few inches from his own. And now they both burst out laughing. But only for a second, for he covered his own mouth while putting his other hand over his brother's. His eyes, however, were still laughing when he jumped under the clothes, and when John Willie impulsively put his arms about him, Davy hugged him to himself, and so, giving each other warmth, they went to sleep.

The next morning, before a flicker of light crept through the boards, John Willie was coughing, and Davy became troubled as he had never been before. He had planned their life ahead feeling they could

survive somehow until he got work, but that would
have been if there was no sickness; he had not taken
into account John Willie's being ill. He felt his head;
it was burning. He couldn't see what he looked like
as yet, but he knew that his brother had a fever.

When he himself had had a fever on him years ago
his mother kept him in bed with a hot brick at his feet
and made him drink hot water with ginger in it. This
had made him sweat and he was soon better. Well, as
soon as it was light he would go to the mine and boil
some water; at least that was free; and perhaps there
might be something to eat on the shelf; who knew?

When the light was breaking he got into some dry
trousers but had to pull on his wet coat and clogs
again. Then with elaborate signs he told John Willie
that he was going to the mine to make a hot drink and
that he had to stay quiet, and should he cough he had
to put his head under the blankets. . . . Did he understand?

John Willie moved his head slowly; his great brown
eyes wide, he stared up at Davy, then brought out a
croaking "Huh."

Peering down at his brother, Davy sighed a deep
sigh; then after giving him one last piece of instruction
by pointing to Snuffy, indicating that he should keep
a tight hold on his lead and that it wouldn't be long
before he himself returned, he went to the side of the
room, pressed the boards away, lay on the floor and
squeezed through the opening. Then after replacing
the boards he moved stealthily through the wet undergrowth and out onto the fells.

The rain had eased somewhat, but he was wet right
through again before he reached the mouth of the
mine. He hurried into the darkness and to the shelf.
. . . There was nothing on it but the utensils and the
blankets. He bit on his lip, stretched out his arm and

took the tinderbox from a niche where he had hidden it and went back to just within the opening, where he made a small fire from the remainder of the dry kindling.

The fire was slow to burn; he blew and blew and almost choked with the smoke before he got it alight. Then after banking it up with more wood, he dashed out and filled the can full of water from the burn. After more puffing and blowing the water had just begun to bubble and he was on the point of lifting the can off the fire when the entrance was darkened by two figures.

Raising his head, he looked up into the faces of Mr. Coxon and Fred.

"Well, well! Gettin' breakfast, lad, eh?"

He made no answer.

"Damp to be outdoors these days, never known so much rain; an' by the look of the sky it's goin' on. Wet winter ahead, I'd say. How's the young 'un standin' up to it?"

"He's standin' up to it all right, Mr. Coxon."

"Well, don't take that attitude, boy; I was only askin' a civil question. Where is he now?"

Where was he now? It was some seconds before he jerked his head and said, "Up there . . . asleep . . . in, in bed. . . . "

"Aw, let's see where he's tucked in."

Davy was on his feet confronting the man. "You mind your own business, Mr. Coxon. I've never asked you for anything, so leave us alone."

"I was only going to have a look at the lad. You said he was in bed. Never heard of a bed in a pit afore, so I'm just curious."

"I . . . I didn't mean bed, not a real bed. I meant— Hie you! come back here."

While they were talking Fred Coxon had slipped past and was running along by the rolley track. Then there came a faint flash of light and his voice came out of the darkness shouting, "Nobody here, da. Couple of blankets, that's all."

Mr. Coxon, his brows raised, his lips pursed into a whistle, looked at Davy; then he said, "Nobody there, lad, only a couple of blankets? Don't tell me you've done him in, that the hump on your back got too heavy for you. . . . Now, now! Don't try any of that, else you'll find yourself lying on your back. But I think this should be gone into, eh? What've you got to say?"

"He's . . . he's farther back."

"Oh, then we'd better have a look farther back, hadn't we?"

Again Davy stepped in front of him. "I told you to mind your own business."

"Aye"—Mr. Coxon's face was grim now—"you did. An' it is me business. Yesterday you had a brother, the day you haven't. If he's not there, where is he? Come on then, tell us."

When Davy remained silent Mr. Coxon turned to his son, who had joined them again, and said, "Fishy business this, Fred; fishy business. We'll go home and have a bite an' then we'd better see into it, hadn't we? It seems like a case for the Justices. Be seein' you, lad. Be seein' you." Mr. Coxon made two ominous movements with his head, then slowly turned away, followed by Fred.

Oh Lord! what now? As if things weren't bad enough. He hated those Coxons, he did. He wished . . . Aw! what was the good of wasting your breath on wishing? He lowered his head onto his chest. He knew what would happen. Mr. Coxon would indeed go to the Justices and take pleasure in it, and when he told them where John Willie was, as he would have to, what would happen then? Oh, he knew what would happen; they'd take John Willie to the House, to the Infirmary as they called it, because he was sick. And he'd have to go in an' all and work for their keep.

Slowly he bent down and took the black can from the fire. After putting the lid on it he reluctantly pressed out the now bright embers with his foot and went out into the rain again. But he didn't run now; he walked with his head down. He had reached bottom. There was nothing more he could do; he'd have to admit defeat. But oh, how he hated, and even feared, the prospect before them.

He went through the hole in the wall and, with his body bent double, through the long grass. He took the boards from the side of the summerhouse and pushed the can through; then, lying flat, as usual, he slithered into the shelter and had risen to his knees when his whole body stiffened and he stared in a petrified fashion at the figure sitting in the basket chair to the side of the mattress on which John Willie still lay.

He never remembered how long he knelt there, or how long the silence lasted as he stared up into the grim visage of Miss Peamarsh.

It was she who spoke first. "Well?" she said; and that was all.

As if easing himself out of a bad cramp he moved one limb after the other and brought himself upright. There was another silence while they still continued to look at each other; and again it was Miss Peamarsh who broke it. Again she said, "Well," but now added, "what have you got to say for yourself this time? And you'd better be quick before I hand you over to the authorities."

What did it matter? What did anything matter? He

couldn't stand much more. Let her do what she liked; let them all do what they liked. His head drooped onto his chest and his voice was utterly weary as he said, "We had no place to go an' I couldn't get work, an' . . . an' I had him to look after. We've done no harm to your hut."

Again there was a silence before Miss Peamarsh said, "You were going to put him into the House the last time we met."

"Aye, I know." He still did not raise his head. "And I might as well have done it then, 'cos it's goin' to happen anyway. Mr. Coxon'll see to that."

"Mr. who?"

He raised his head a little and looked at her under his lids as he said with deep sarcasm, "A friend, a neighbor, Mr. Coxon. We used to live near him. He's still got his house; he's a blackleg."

His head came up just a little more when she said, "Coxon? Well, Coxon was always the blackleg type, if I remember rightly."

She remembered Coxon. Of course she'd remember everybody in the row, and in the village, and roundabout for miles, because she had been the parson's daughter and had done good works, giving out soup and clothes and things like that. His mother had told him. Well, there was only one good thing that had happened this morning: there was somebody besides himself who didn't like Coxon. He could pick up that much from her tone.

"You know this boy is very ill?"

"I don't need to be told that."

"Don't you dare speak to me in that tone of voice. And address me as miss when you do speak." She was on her feet now and they were glaring at each other.

Then, his head drooping again, he said, "I'm sorry,

miss, I am, I am that, but . . . but I've come to the end of me tether. Mr. Coxon'll be routing us out with the Justices shortly. He thinks I've done him in." He nodded down to John Willie, whose wide eyes were fixed on him. "I . . . I couldn't tell him he was in here, else he would have split on me. Well—" he made a sound like a disdainful laugh and ended, "it's as broad as it's long, isn't it? Whichever way it goes he'll have the satisfaction of seeing us goin' to the House."

"He doesn't like you then . . . Coxon?"

"No. Nor me him. Nor any of the tribe."

They were looking at each other again but not so fiercely now, and he watched her head bobbing in small movements. Then, swinging round, she looked down on John Willie and said, "Can you carry him?"

"Carry him? Where? It's still raining and he's got the cough on him. If we can wait here till the . . ."

She was glaring at him again. "I asked you a simple question. Are you able to carry him wrapped up in the blankets?"

"Aye, aye, I'm able to carry him."

"Then set about it and follow me. Go on!" She made a sharp flicking movement with her fingers.

He didn't immediately respond but asked, "Where . . . where'll I carry him?"

"Are you stupid, boy? Didn't I say follow me?"

"You . . . you wouldn't put him outside, not in this?"

He watched her close her eyes; then, her tone changing just the slightest, she said, "What I'm saying, boy, is for you to bring him to the house where there's warmth, that is if you don't want him to die. . . . Do you want him to die?"

What could he answer? And so he answered nothing, but almost springing on John Willie, he rolled him

in the blankets, hoisted him up, then, stumbling somewhat, followed Miss Peamarsh through the narrow
open door down the two grass-strewn steps. And
Snuffy came close on his heels.

She had said nothing about the dog, and a section
of Davy's mind panicked at the thought of what would
happen when Snuffy passed the geese.

But nothing happened—that is, nothing that he expected to happen—because when the geese, their
necks stretched out, started honking, Davy was
amazed to see the dog giving them a wide berth.

Davy's arms were almost giving way when, still following the tall, thin, striding figure, he entered the
kitchen of the house.

"Lay him down there."

Obediently he laid John Willie on the padded seat
of a wooden settle that stood to the side of the black
range, wherein glowed the biggest fire he had seen for
many a day.

"Sit yourself down."

Obediently again, he lowered himself slowly down
onto the end of the settle. And now his weary, amazed
gaze watched Miss Peamarsh throw off her hood and
cloak, then take a pan and half fill it with water from
the pump in the corner of the kitchen, place it on the
fire and throw into it three handfuls of oatmeal, after
which she brought from a delf rack a platter with a loaf
on it and another holding a square of butter, then a
bowl full to the top with milk. From this she filled a
jug. Then she marched out of the room and left them
alone.

As if he were still in a dream Davy looked around
the kitchen. It was an enormous room and he was
amazed at the comfort of it . . . and at the cleanliness.

She must clean it herself, and she a lady. Finally, he turned his head and looked on John Willie. The boy's eyes were closed as if he were asleep, and his usually pale skin was a high red color.

The door opened and in marched Miss Peamarsh again. She had a bottle in one hand and she picked up a spoon from the table and came to the settle, saying to Davy without looking at him, "Raise him up." And Davy lifted John Willie up.

"Tell him to open his mouth."

Davy tapped on his brother's lips. Then Miss Peamarsh poured a spoonful of the liquid into John Willie's open mouth. She did it slowly, even gently, but when John Willie screwed up his face against the taste she said harshly, "Nonsense! Nonsense! Another one."

"There now!" she exclaimed when John Willie had swallowed the second teaspoonful. "There now!" Then she went to the fire, stirred the pot while saying, "It won't be long; overcooking spoils porridge," and turned her head and looked straight at Davy, adding, "Do you know that?"

"No, miss."

"No, of course you don't; your people stick it in the oven all night and leave it to set like glue."

Some minutes later she poured out two plates of porridge, covering them with the thick creamy milk before indicating with a movement of her hand that Davy should come to the table and eat.

Slowly he rose and went and sat down by the table, but he did not start immediately and gulp at the wondrous meal before him; instead he looked to where Miss Peamarsh, after propping John Willie up against the end of the settle, was feeding him with a spoon.

There arose in Davy that awful feeling again, the feeling that made his eyes smart and brought a lump into his gullet. He began spooning the porridge up rapidly, until Miss Peamarsh's voice hit him like a stone, saying, "Don't gollop, boy! Take it slowly, or you too will be ill."

"Yes, miss. . . . Yes, miss."

Two minutes later his plate was clean; but not John Willie's. After only a few spoonfuls John Willie had shaken his head and Miss Peamarsh had not pressed him to take more. Now, standing at the far end of the table, she looked at Davy, and he, seeing she was about to speak, rose to his feet.

"Well, what now?"

"I . . . I don't know, miss, except that Mr. Coxon'll be along shortly. I know he won't waste no time."

She stared at him, her lips tight; then she turned and looked to where John Willie was lying once again with his eyes closed, his breathing now audible. Bringing her eyes back to Davy, she said, "You know that if he goes into the House it'll be the finish of him, even if he survives the journey there?"

"You . . . you think he's that bad, miss?"

"Of course he's that bad. He must have been bad for days; haven't you noticed?"

"No, not until he started coughin' yesterday."

As they stared at each other a silence fell on the kitchen, broken only by the sound of the pattering rain and John Willie's heavy breathing.

Her next words so amazed him that he too was struck dumb, because what she said to him was, "I'll allow you to stay here until he's fully recovered. . . . Did you hear what I said, boy? . . ."

"Aye. Ye . . . yes, miss." He wanted to sit down, but

instead he grabbed the edge of the table. He wasn't going to pass out, was he? Eeh! he felt funny.

"Sit yourself down." She was standing over him, but she didn't touch him, and he lowered himself onto the chair again. Then looking up at her, he said in a whisper, "You mean it, miss?"

"I'm not in the habit of saying things I don't mean. But don't you imagine it's going to be easy. You haven't fallen on what you would term a soft spot, you understand that?"

"Aye, yes, miss. Oh, I'll work. I'll do anything; anything. Clean up the whole place."

"Clean up the whole place? What do you mean?"

"Well, miss, I mean just the rough parts, just the . . ."

"You'll do what you're told and nothing more."

"Yes, miss. Yes, miss." He nodded slowly at her.

She turned from him now and walked to the fire, where she stood, her back straight, her hand extended out and up toward the high mantelpiece, and although she was speaking to him she seemed to be talking to herself as she said, "There's rooms above the stables; they were inhabitated at one time. The roof is sound; there is furniture still there; the place just needs cleaning up. But before we go over there you must change your clothes. Have you any dry clothes?"

"No, no, miss. The others are wet an' all; they're back in the hut . . . summerhouse."

She turned now and faced him but didn't move away from the fire, and her voice was low and her words slow as she said, "You will go and bring all your possessions from . . . from the summerhouse. You will put the door back into place and you will not—I repeat, you will not—go into it again or into that part of the garden. You fully understand that?"

He stared at her a moment before answering, "Yes, miss."

"Fully? . . . I said fully. You understand that you are not to go into that part of the garden again?"

"Yes, yes, I understand, miss."

"What are you to do?"

"Clear our things out of the . . . summerhouse, close the door, and not go into that part of the garden again."

"When I give an order I expect it to be obeyed."

"Aye . . . I understand, miss."

"Very well, go now and bring the rest of your things; we must see to having them dried."

Like one in a dream Davy went out of the house and across the rough lawn and through the undergrowth to the summerhouse, and he gathered up their belongings. Then he pulled the swaying door closed behind him, and not once did he ask himself why she was so emphatic about his not going into this part of the garden again, for if any part wanted clearing this part did. He was so dazed at what had happened to them that it wasn't worth bothering about.

When he returned to the kitchen Davy was amazed to see that John Willie was no longer lying on the couch but in a sort of basket bed-chair, and moreover he was dressed in what looked, from the upper part of him, like a big white nightshirt, for although the sleeves were rolled up his thin arms were lost in them. Miss Peamarsh was covering him over with blankets, and not their blankets but big cream-colored ones. She turned her head and looked at Davy. "Well!" she began again. "Don't stand there gaping. Have you put your things up in the rooms?"

"No, miss; I . . . I don't know where they are."

"No, no, of course not. Your things . . . where are they?"

"In the porch, miss."

She turned again to John Willie, and now she wagged her finger at him as she said, "Lie still. I'll soon be back."

"He . . . he can't hear you, miss."

"I know he can't hear me; you have already informed me he is deaf and dumb; but nevertheless, as he seems to understand you, he will understand me."

She marched across the kitchen now and lifted her cloak from the back of the door, saying, "Come along then," but stopped abruptly as the sound of a bell clanging in the distance came to them.

Davy looked at her, at her profile. She was standing straight and stiff, and if he hadn't known that Miss Peamarsh was afraid of nothing or nobody he would have said that the expression on her face showed apprehension, if not fear. But that was silly. Nevertheless, he saw that she was disturbed by the sound of the bell, which must be coming from the main gate.

"Who is it?" She turned and looked at him as if he could tell her. "I'm expecting no one. It isn't the day for the grocery cart; it's not due until next week; and—" She turned her head slowly and looked around the room, and Davy was about to say, "Will I go, miss, and see who it is?" when she said abruptly, "Stay where you are. Don't move now." And then she almost ran across the kitchen and out of the far door like a young girl or a young woman would. But she was no young girl; as for a young woman, he shook his head at the thought; she was old. Going by his ma's reckoning she should be all of thirty-five.

He raised his eyes upward as he heard her footsteps

on the stairs. There seemed to be a lot of stairs. When he could no longer hear them, he looked across at John Willie. And John Willie was looking at him. He smiled at him and raised his hand and waved as if a great distance separated them, and John Willie smiled in return and after a moment's hesitation raised his hand, too, a little way from the blankets.

The sound of her footsteps again on the stairs brought Davy's eyes to the door once more, and when Miss Peamarsh entered, there was a different expression on her face, which he couldn't put a name to either, only to think that his ma would have said she looked like the cat that had licked the cream.

She came right up to him before she spoke. "Do you know who's at the gate?"

"No, miss." He shook his head in perplexity.

"Your friend."

"Me friend?"

"Yes, Coxon."

"Mr. Coxon?"

"That's who I said, Coxon. What do you think he's come for?"

Davy knew what he had come for. He moved his head from side to side before answering, "He . . . he must have watched me, an' saw where I came in. This morning in the mine when I was boiling the water, he . . . he came up an' taunted me an' almost accused me of doin' John Willie"—he nodded toward the chair— "of doing him in. . . . "

He stopped speaking and was amazed now to see another change come over her face. The color had drained from her cheeks and her lower lip was actually trembling, so much so that she pressed her teeth into it.

He blinked up at her. What was wrong with her?

"You all right, miss?" Quickly now he reassured her, "I . . . I would never do anything like that, miss, not to our John Willie; nor nobody else, for that matter. I . . . I'm fond of our John Willie. It was Coxon's bad mind. He . . . he said John Willie was like a hump on me back and I'd have to carry him all me life and . . ."

"Be quiet, boy!"

"Yes, miss."

"Now—" Her hand was across the top of her chest. She began to pat it as she said, "Well now, what shall we say to your friend?"

"He's no friend of mine, miss."

"Well then, what shall we say to Coxon, for as you say he's likely watched you come into the grounds. And by the way"—her finger was wagging at him now—"I want to know exactly how you did get in. We'll deal with that later, but what shall we say to Mr. Coxon now?"

She had stressed the mister in such a way that he smiled faintly at her as he answered, "We'll say I've been taken into your employ, Miss Peamarsh."

"Well put, boy. Well put. But we'll let him have his say first. Come along. But do not accompany me down the drive. There is a path behind the hedge that leads to the gates; you take that. I shall call you when I wish you to appear."

As if now he were joining in a game, he grinned at her and said, "Aye, miss. Aye, miss."

"Come, then." She made for the door, but there she turned and once more wagged her finger toward John Willie. Then she went out, and Davy followed her, being careful to keep a step or two behind and to the left of her, for he knew his place.

When they came to the front of the house and

crossed the drive, she turned and pointed silently toward the path she had mentioned, and as silently he nodded at her, then scurried down it toward the gates.

Before reaching the end of the path, he stopped where it turned and let onto the drive. From here he had a view of the gate and was also within hearing distance. He saw Miss Peamarsh come to a stop about two feet from the gate, and then he heard her now familiar "Well!"

"Good-day to you, Miss Peamarsh." Mr. Coxon's voice sounded oily; he had taken his cap off and was holding it in both hands. "I've come to tell you somethin' that I think you should know about. Although it won't please you, I think you should know about it."

"You have come to tell me something that won't please me but you think I should know about? Well, get on with it, man, and tell me."

"It's about young Halladay, a boy called Davy Halladay, and his idiot brother. Although I'd like to state, miss, at this point I'm not sure about the whereabouts of the brother, but as for him I know that he's got into your grounds through a hole in the bottom of your wall, an' I thought it was my rightful duty to put you wise, miss."

"He came into my grounds through a hole in the wall, you say, Coxon?"

"Yes, miss. I saw the place with me own eyes. I followed him this very mornin'."

"Really! Really! I'm surprised that he should use the hole in the wall when there is a gate to come through."

Davy now saw her thrust out her hand and grip a bar of the iron gate and shake it vigorously. Then his eyes stretched wide at her next words.

"David Halladay is no stupid individual; there must have been a good reason why he used the hole in the wall."

There was a pause before Matthew Coxon said, "I . . . I don't quite follow you, miss."

"No, you don't follow me, *Mister* Coxon, but you followed the boy. You followed him in order to deprive him, as you thought, of shelter; shelter that you did not think of offering him yourself, a workmate and a neighbor as I understand he was of yours. You let him go on the road and be responsible for a sick and afflicted child. Well, *Mister* Coxon, I want to inform you that your kindly act in coming to tell me that my grounds are being used to shelter vagrants is quite misplaced. Furthermore, I will inform you that David Halladay is in my employ, and if he used the hole in the wall, it was likely only to cut short a journey round to these gates."

There was another pause, and Davy actually heard Matthew Coxon splutter before saying, "You . . . you've taken him on?" and now all servility was gone from his tone as he added, "Late in the day, isn't it, miss, for you to employ anybody an' the place gone to rack and ruin these many a year? An' it's been a lightning engagement if I know owt, for the last time I saw him he was at his wits' end."

"To answer your last statement first, Mr. Coxon, I will say that that boy could never come to his wits' end. He's much too resourceful; he'll always have wits to fall back upon. As for my grounds going to rack and ruin, that is my business. And I will remind you, Coxon, to keep your place and remember whom you're addressing. And finally, as for the younger boy, he's in bed at present with a cold. Are you satisfied?"

There was another pause before Coxon replied,

"You want an answer, miss? Well, I'll tell you. No, I'm not satisfied; there's somethin' fishy here. You can't pull the wool over my eyes no more than that young scut can; you don't take in people like those two as sharp as a crack of a gun without reason."

"And you intend to find out the reason, Mr. Coxon? Is that what you are implying? Well, you have my permission; you are welcome to probe into my motives in engaging David Halladay and his brother . . ."

"Huh! an' his brother!"

Davy's amazement stretching his face, he watched Matthew Coxon and Miss Peamarsh glaring at each other through the iron bars of the gate. Not until Mr. Coxon had turned away and marched off down the road did Miss Peamarsh leave the gate, and then she too marched up the drive, and as she did so he ran up the narrow path and met her as she emerged onto the grass-strewn gravel in front of the house. But before he had time to speak, she wiped the smile from his face by saying, "Yes, you heard it all, but everything I said about you was exaggeration on my part. As yet I know nothing about your merits; what I said to him was merely to put him in his place and help to pay off an old score, so don't imagine, boy, you're dealing with someone soft in the head. You understand me?"

Understand her? He would never understand her; she was a strange one. No, he didn't understand her; giving him shelter, feeding him, taking his part against old Coxon, then saying she was just doing it to pay off an old score. . . . She was a funny 'un.

"Now to look at the rooms. . . . And don't walk behind me, boy; I am not a mother duck, nor the Bishop of Durham."

It was at this point that Davy almost burst out laughing. He had just thought she was a funny 'un, and now here she was proving to be funny in more ways than one. And of a sudden he knew that he was no longer afraid of her; and because he admitted this to himself, he realized that he had also admitted that he had been afraid of her.

They came to the stables, and as they passed them and made for the door to the side she indicated them with a movement of her hand, saying, "That is Florence's apartment. You have made the acquaintance of Florence?" She was staring down at him with a sideward glance.

"Florence?" He screwed up his eyes at her.

"Yes, Florence, the cow."

"Yes. Oh, aye!"

When she found some difficulty in opening the door that led to the rooms above the cowshed, he put his shoulder to it and pressed it inward, then stood aside, and she passed him without comment and went up the dark stairs, and he followed her.

"Well, these are they. There are three rooms. This one as you see has a fireplace; it's quite a good fireplace, big. There's a griddle bar"—she was pointing now—"and a hook for your kettle. Everything as you can see is very rusty, but the roof is sound."

He followed her gaze upward where the wooden rafters lay exposed, and he saw that the roof was sound, although it was hanging in cobwebs. But what were cobwebs! There was rising in him like a tide a feeling of joy. He could see the place when it was cleaned up. By! it would be grand and cozy. Forgetting Miss Peamarsh for a moment, he hurried to the window. It looked down onto the yard and the back door of the house. It was really all part of the house, the stables and these rooms and the coal house and the wood shed forming a right angle to it.

He turned to her. She was looking intently at him with yet another expression on her face now, an unguarded expression, for at the moment he did not seem to recognize her, she looked so different. Or perhaps it was himself who was feeling different. He could never remember feeling so excited as he did at this moment.

"It's grand, miss. Thank you. Thank you from the bottom of me heart. I'll . . . I'll clean it up. . . ."

"Don't start thanking me in words, boy. I want actions, deeds, work."

"You'll have them, miss. From dawn till dark you'll have them."

Again he saw that look on her face before she turned from him, saying abruptly now, "You must scrub everything; tables, chairs, dresser, everything." She moved into another room, saying, "Here is the bed. As you see it's iron and brass. Its spring is rusty but it's still whole. I will give you a mattress from the house, that is"—she nodded at him sternly now— "when that spring is clean enough to take it."

All he did now was to nod at her.

"This other room is very small." She had thrust open a door off the little landing. "It is merely a box room, but you could use it to store wood."

Again he nodded, but now his mind was saying, "Store wood? What did you store wood for, the winter?" He would not allow his thoughts to go any further, then almost jumped as she barked, "Don't stand there gaping. Let us get back to your brother, then you take soap and water and start right away. Understand?"

"Yes, miss."

The feeling of joy was still with him, even as he thought. By! she's going to be a tartar. And she seemed to start everything with, *"Well!"* and finish with *"You understand?"* Still, he was grateful to her, as he had said, from the bottom of his heart, and thankful to God also, to all the gods. Eeh! why had he said that last bit? It sounded like swearin'; holy swearin'. Then he remembered that the ginger-headed man had said that: "Not all the gods will get the better of me."

Four

It took Davy three days of sweeping and scrubbing
before the rooms were habitable.

Miss Peamarsh had told him to light a fire each day
in order to air the place. This he had done, and now
everything was ready for him and John Willie to move
in. His final touch to the living room was to unwrap
the jug from the old shirt and place it on the mantelpiece. Then he stood back from it, his head on one
side, surveying it with pride as if he had just created
it himself. It looked lovely, better than it ever had on
the mantelpiece at home, because there it had been
crowded on both sides with odds and ends.

He took the last bucket of dirty water downstairs
and emptied it in the cesspool that lay to the side of
what had once been the vegetable garden. Miss Peamarsh had warned him that no matter what the
weather, slops must be emptied into the cesspool.

Then going to the pump that stood at the end of the yard he washed his hands, afterward rubbing them over his hair, which action served two purposes: it helped to dry them and at the same time to make his head look tidy.

The twilight was deepening as he crossed the yard. He knocked on the kitchen door, and when he was asked to enter he opened the door but stopped for a moment, the door handle still in his hand, as he took in the scene before him. John Willie was lying propped up in the chair-bed that was still placed before the fire, and Miss Peamarsh was sitting to the side of the fireplace facing him, and she was sewing by the light of the lamp. There was a smell of fresh bread in the kitchen, which added to the homely scene. He could never associate Miss Peamarsh with the word homely, yet everything in this room at this moment was homely.

"Well!" She turned her head and glanced at him.

"I've finished the place, miss. Everything's ready, all . . . all but the mattress goin' up."

"It's for me to say when everything's ready. Light the lantern and I will take a look."

"Yes, miss."

He now went to a side table where stood two lanterns and proceeded to light one of them. During the process he glanced across the room at John Willie.

John Willie seemed to be waiting for his look, because he immediately smiled at him and, without raising his arm from the coverlet, twiddled his fingers at him, which action Davy saw did not go unnoticed by Miss Peamarsh, who had risen and was folding up her sewing.

She did not put her cloak on when she went out now, because the day had been dry, but as she always did when leaving the room she turned and wagged her finger at John Willie, and in return John Willie smiled at her.

Davy had pondered a great deal during these past three days on the relationship that had sprung up between their John Willie and this woman; this strange woman, this woman who would bark his head off one minute, then show him a kindness the next, such as heaping his plate with food. He had never tasted such food as she gave him. Although he had seen no meat in the house, there was an abundance of eggs and cheese, butter and milk, and the things she did with them continued to amaze him. Last night for his supper she had given him a big baked potato split down the middle and running with melted cheese. Eeh! he had never tasted anything like it before. He'd had baked taties, yes, but not running with hot cheese. And then she made custard with eggs; it tasted wonderful. She stuffed John Willie every day with this custard made with eggs. It seemed strange to him that a lady—and no matter what her manner, no matter how she dressed, no matter how she looked, nobody could deny that she still remained a lady—should clean her own house and look after poultry and a cow, and muck them out at that. But he had seen her do it. And he had made up his mind that once he had finished cleaning the rooms she would do no more mucking out, not as long as he was here.

"Stop your dreaming." Her hand flicked out toward him with her usual gesture. "Come along."

He followed her out and across the yard and up the stairs and into the main room. She took the lantern from him and, holding it up, examined the walls, then the table and the chairs, the small wooden settle and the cupboard, whose doors she opened and along whose shelves she ran her fingers; then she turned and looked toward the fireplace, and her eyes lifted to the jug on the mantelpiece. They remained there for a moment before, moving slowly toward it, she picked it up and examined it. Now looking at Davy, she asked sternly, "Where did you get this?"

"From home, miss."

"From home?"

"Yes, miss. It . . . it belonged to me grannie. 'Twas given to her on her wedding day by the people she worked for."

Miss Peamarsh now put down the lantern and held the jug in both hands, and then, her voice quite soft, she said, "Do you understand the value of this jug, boy?"

"No, miss; only that it's old."

"Only that it's old!" she repeated, and shook her head slightly, then added, "Indeed it is old. If I am not mistaken it is one of the early Chelsea pieces. You have seen the name on the bottom?"

"Yes . . . no, miss. I mean yes, but I didn't know what it meant."

"No, of course." A semblance of her usual tone crept back into her voice. "You cannot read. But this"—again her tone was low and soft—"this piece could be worth a lot of money."

"Really, miss!"

"Yes."

"How much do you reckon, miss . . . more than a pound?"

He watched her swallow before she spoke again; then she said, "Yes, more than a pound. I am not an expert on china, but I know a little about it, and I should say if it was taken to the proper source you would get a good sum for it."

"Well, well." Unconsciously he used her term, then he ran his forefinger along the bottom of his nose and smiled at her as he said, "We were starvin' and we had the jug and we didn't know. I would have been glad to have taken a shilling for it. Funny, isn't it, miss?"

"Indeed it is funny, boy." She was examining it again, and now she asked, "How have you managed to carry it about with you and not break it?"

"Oh, I kept it wrapped up in a hanky and John Willie carried it. He's careful. Although he's not strong, he's careful."

She was nodding at him now, and, her voice still soft, she said, "Yes, I should imagine he's careful."

She turned away and slowly placed the jug on the mantelpiece again. And now he asked her, "Is everythin' all right—I mean to your satisfaction, miss?"

"Yes." She glanced round the room once more. "You have done your work well, but you will not be able to move your brother here for some days. He is much better, but he's still a sick child. I think he should remain where he is for another week."

She had her back to him as she spoke, and he said, "Just as you say, miss. . . . And, miss, can I say somethin'?"

She turned toward him again. "Well?"

"It's just this, miss. Can I take it on meself to do the mucking out from the morrow mornin'? An' then I could start diggin' what was the vegetable garden. You could grow lots of stuff in there, miss, your own taties and such, and swedes and the like. And then there's the currant bushes. I could clear round . . ."

She cut him off abruptly by saying, "I will give you permission to clear the vegetable garden, but as I told you before I do not want the north side of the land touched at all. I . . . I prefer to leave it growing wild.

Anyway, the fruit trees and bushes are old. What is required is a new stock, and if you clear enough land around the vegetable garden, that's what we'll do—plant a new stock. Understand?"

"Aye, miss, yes, yes, I understand. And I'll do that."

Holding the lantern high, he lit her way down the stairs and across the yard, and when they were in the kitchen once more she went straight to the chair-bed and with fussing movements began to straighten and tuck the clothes around John Willie, and he lay there looking at her, his eyes wide and smiling as if he knew her well and liked her, and as he looked at them Davy recalled their first meeting when John Willie had appeared to like her right away. It was funny about the pair of them, how they had taken to each other—not laughing funny, but odd funny.

He was standing waiting to be told what next to do when, straightening her back, she suddenly said, "Sit down."

He went and sat on the chair she pointed to. It was at the other side of John Willie's bed, and she, seating herself at the foot of it, arranged the skirt of her dress, which today was a gray one and made her look altogether different from when she wore the old black serge skirt and blouse and the weather-stained cloak. She brought his eyes wide now by saying, "In future I shall call you David."

He said nothing to this. What could he say? But he could answer her next question. "How much did you earn when you worked down the mine?"

"Oh, well, miss . . . it differed like. A good wage could be sixteen shillings. . . ."

"A week?" Her face was screwed up in disbelief.

And he said on a laugh, "No, miss, a fortnight. We always got paid by the fortnight. But on some bad weeks it could be as little as four and six a week, an' . . ."

She nodded now toward John Willie.

"Oh, he never earned anythin', miss; they wouldn't bond him—he was too puny."

"Scandalous. However you look at it, scandalous."

He nodded silently at her, then murmured, "Yes, miss, scandalous."

"Well, boy . . . David, I can assure you there will never come a time when you will earn sixteen shillings a fortnight in my employ, nor yet as far as I can see at this moment four and six a week. I want you to understand that clearly now."

"Yes, miss, I do, I do, and I'm . . ."

" . . . Don't stress the fact that you're willing to work for nothing. That is the talk of a hungry man, or boy, or animal." At this she cast her glance down to where Snuffy was lying stretched out across the mat in front of the fire. "And that's another thing, the animal's name. It is an objectionable name for a dog, or any other animal, Snuffy. We shall call him Rex. From now on we shall call him Rex. Understand?"

Well, she might call him Rex—she could call him what she liked—and he would likely have to call him Rex when she was there, but he'd always remain Snuffy to him.

"As I was saying, with regard to wages, I cannot promise you more than two shillings a week at the most. Now, now"—her finger was raised again—"don't say you'll be quite content with that for life, because I won't believe you. For as soon as the child has regained full strength and the winter is over, the mine and big wages will call you."

Eeh! the mine calling him. If she only knew how he dreaded going down below again. And big wages.

Eeh! big wages, she said. Although four and six a week wasn't to be sneezed at, he had never considered it enough for sixty hours' work. But let her go on. He had discovered she liked talkin'. It was likely because she had spent so much time on her own, with nobody to talk to.

"However, this will be supplemented by your food and your house and"—she paused here—"your education."

His mouth dropped into a gape; his eyes stretched wide. "Education, miss?"

"That's what I said, education. I propose to teach you to read and write, and in the process I hope to impart an understanding of letters to . . . to the child here." Her hand flicked again, indicating John Willie, who had eased himself up and was staring from one to the other as if he could follow what they were saying.

Now Davy's face fell into a relaxed smile and he said slowly, "You'll learn me to read and write, miss?"

"No, I shall not *learn* you to read and write—only you can *learn*—but I shall teach you to read and write. Understand?"

Again he didn't understand—well, not really, only that there must be some difference between learn and teach, but at the moment he couldn't see it. Nevertheless, the prospect was exciting. He said with eagerness, "I'll be able to write me name, miss?"

"I should hope so, and much more than that. And if one makes up one's mind to do a thing, there is no time like the present. Procrastination is the thief of time. Did you know that?"

"N . . . no, miss."

She rose from the chair now, saying, "Stay where you are until I return."

And he stayed. But once she had left the room he

drew his chair close to the bed and, taking hold of John Willie's hand, bent over him and whispered, "All right?" And, as though he had heard, John Willie made two deep movements with his head, then clasped Davy's hand tight, and with one of those gestures that always had the throat-tightening effect on Davy, he brought the hand to his cheek and held it there.

When Davy heard the sound of Miss Peamarsh's steps approaching the door, he pulled a face, gave a little jerk with his head, then pushed the chair back to its former position.

Miss Peamarsh entered the kitchen, now carrying another lamp. She did not speak while she lit it with a spill from the fire, but when it was glowing she lifted it up, saying, "Come along," and, obedient as always, Davy followed her, noting that this time she did not wag her finger in John Willie's direction, probably because they weren't leaving the house.

He had never been beyond the kitchen, and when he stepped into the hall he saw that it was a fine place, half paneled and with oak stairs leading up from the middle of it. In the bobbing light from the lamp he saw pictures of men and women high up on the walls. And that was all he could take in before he mounted the stairs.

When they reached the upper floor he found himself on a landing bigger than the room that they had lived in at home. There were doors going off on all sides and at the far end another flight of stairs; these were narrower and steeper, and the landing they came onto now was small. There were only two doors on this landing. When Miss Peamarsh opened the one to her right, Davy saw that they were in a long narrow attic room that must have run the length of the house.

Miss Peamarsh now placed the lamp on a wooden

table, at each end of which stood two straight-backed chairs. Without a word she went to a set of shelves which held row after row of books, and from the bottom shelf she took three big ones and brought them to the table. When she laid them down Davy saw that the cloth covers were ragged as if from use or mishandling.

He watched her now go to the far corner of the room where some boxes were stacked. After opening three, she brought the third one to the table, saying, "This will do for the present. Like a five-year-old child you will start at the bottom and work upward, and . . ." She stopped abruptly and slowly looked around the room, in a way, Davy thought, as a stranger might, as he himself had done, not having seen it before. Then in a tone of voice that was new to him she said, "This was our nursery and the schoolroom." She brought her eyes to rest on him and repeated, "It was our schoolroom."

"Was it, miss?"

"Yes." Again her eyes roamed around the room. "Many years ago it was our schoolroom."

For a moment he had a picture of her and her brother, the one who had gone to foreign parts, sitting as children at this table learning their letters. But as she said, it was a long time ago.

"Take up the books and this box." Her voice sounded sad to him now, and he lifted up the things from the table and followed her.

In the kitchen once more, she turned out the contents of the box onto the table, and he saw a jumbled mass of inch-high letters and numbers. And now she said, "Help me pull the child's bed toward the table."

As he went to lift the head of the chair-bed and she the foot, she stopped in her stooped position; and, looking along the length of it over John Willie toward him, she said, "He is not stupid, this child."

"I know he's not, miss. I've always said that."

"Then we mustn't treat him as if he were stupid, must we?"

"No, miss." His tone was slightly on the defensive. He would have liked to add, "I never have," but he held his peace. She thought she had discovered something about John Willie all on her own, and it would do no harm to let her think so.

They sat down at the table now, he on the same side as John Willie and she facing them both. Opening the worn books at the first page, she handed the first one to John Willie and then the other to him, after which she selected a letter from the table, held it up, then pointing alternately to the first letter in both books she said, "A." Her eyes now on Davy, she demanded, "Say A. Say after me, A." Then, her voice harsh, she cried out, "Don't look at the child! He will follow. Pay attention to what I say. That letter is A. Say A."

"A."

"Not like that; it isn't Aa, it is A. Say hay."

"Hay."

"That's right. Now say A."

"Hay."

"No, A."

"A."

"That's better. Now B."

"B."

So this was what was called education; this was how you learned to write your name. It went on for an hour. A, then B, then C, then D, then E. He had a lot of trouble with E; it was as bad as the A. He didn't know now whether he was going to like education, and whether it was worth all this just to be able to write your name. But like it or not, he'd have to stick to it if only to please her, and he wanted to please her. It was funny, but apart from everything else, the job, the roof over their heads, their bellies full, he wanted to please her.

Five

His ma used to say if they went a week without trouble of some kind or another, life was too good to be true; and this was brought home to Davy during his third week in Miss Peamarsh's employment.

Everything seemed to happen in that third week, and looking back on it, it all connected up, one thing with the other.

The first thing that happened was pleasant, for he was able to give a hand to someone worse off than himself.

He had suggested to Miss Peamarsh that he should do something about the front gates—get the rust off them and clear the grass that was growing about their feet. He was taking a pride in the place; he saw that it could be a handsome house and a beautiful garden if all were fixed up. He couldn't see himself really getting to the bottom of it, but he could clear the main

parts, and in his estimation you judged a house by its
entrance.

So it was on a day that was cold and dull that he saw
a tall figure pass by the gates. He would have let the
man go unnoticed, for he himself was at the side hidden by a pillar, but he saw the red hair sticking from
under the black cap and hanging over the turned-up
collar and he recognized the man from the workhouse,
the man who had done a bunk. "Hie there!" he called.

The man turned and looked toward the gates, then
came hurrying forward. "Why, hello, lad," he said.
"What you doing in there?"

"I've . . . I've been hired by Miss Peamarsh."

"Miss Peamarsh? You mean the old eccentric
woman? I've heard tell of her; what's she like?"

"Well, for a start she's not all that old, and . . . and
she's not what they say—you know, funny like. No, not
a bit; she's all right really."

"Well, well. And she's hired you for good?"

"Aw well, I'm not sure of that, but for the winter
anyway. An' we've got rooms. And . . . and she looked
after John Willie. He was bad, right bad. We were
sleepin' out in her summerhouse an' she found us."
He shrugged his shoulders now up above his ears. "I
thought me end had come, but she took us in and she
nursed him, John Willie, and he's fine now. And you
know what? He's gettin' fat. . . . Well, not fat, but he's
putting on weight. Eeh! the milk he drinks. And you
know something else? She's learning me me letters.
I can do me name now an' I'll soon be able to read."

"By, that's wonderful; that's the best news yet.
You'll never be really lonely if you can read, lad."

"Can you read?"

"Yes; and write, thank God. I always carry a book
around with me—at least I have done up till lately."

The tall man now shook his head and smiled, saying quietly, "I'm glad for you, lad. In all ways I'm glad for you. It's a change to hear something good happening to somebody these days."

"You've never got hired anywhere?"

"No, I've traveled miles since I saw you. The farther you go the worse things are, so I came back here a few days ago. I'm camping out in the old mine. You know, just yonder over the fells. I found a couple of blankets and a pan and odds and ends. Someone must have been . . ."

"Oh, I'm glad it was you. I went back an' found they were gone. I . . . I thought it was a onetime neighbor of ours who's got it in for me. I thought one of his lads had been and took them."

"They belong to you, lad?"

"Aye, but I don't need them anymore; you're welcome to them. But you said you were in the mine?"

"Yes, I am, but farther in. I found a shelf that's pretty dry."

"Oh, I'm glad."

As they looked at each other, a feeling almost of guilt assailed Davy. The man's cheeks were hollow, and he was not old but youngish. Early thirties, he thought, yet his face looked gaunt. Impulsively he thrust his hands into his back pocket and after a bit of fumbling unpinned the little leather pouch in which he carried his pay. It was through habit that he carried what money he had on him. Unless you were a fool you never left money about, not even if you had a house, because that could be broken into. There were four whole shillings in his bag, and he took two out and handed them through the bars to the man. But the man didn't take them. He stared down at the coins and, shaking his head, said, "No, lad, no, I couldn't.

You must have had to work hard for that. Thanks all the same.''

And Davy, pushing his hands farther through the bars, said, "Look, man, I've got everything I want here; I eat so much food it's coming out of me ears. Go on; you can pay me back if you like when you get set on.''

He watched the man moving his lips tightly over each other, and when his hand came slowly forward he did not immediately take the shillings but gripped Davy's hand between both of his as he said, "Thanks, lad. I don't know how, but someday I'll pay you back; in some way I'll pay you back. That's a promise. And I can say in this minute that miracles do happen. I was nearing the end of me tether. Aye''—he shook his head and smiled—"miracles do happen. Thanks again, lad.''

"You're welcome. An' will I be seeing you if you're staying around here?''

"Yes, lad, you'll be seeing me, if it's only to pay you interest on this.'' He held out his palm, which was visibly trembling, then turned abruptly away and went off down the road.

Davy watched him through the gate. Eeh! he must be near starving. If only he could give him half the food that he got. He liked his grub, nobody better, but she piled his plate up, then gave him second helpings. If only he could smuggle some out. But he'd better not; she'd be mad at him if she found him doing that. But she couldn't stop him doing what he liked with his pay, could she? No, because that was his own. She had said they were free to go out every Sunday. Well, next Sunday he'd go to the mine. Aye, he would. That's what he'd do, he'd go to the mine and see him again, 'cos he liked that fellow. Aye; aye, he did.

The next thing that happened was heralded by the bell.

It was odd, he thought, but Miss Peamarsh always looked startled when she heard the bell. He and John Willie had just returned to the house and entered the kitchen. They had been looking for Snuffy. Two or three times during the last week he had disappeared, and what was more, he had stopped eating the way he used to.

Miss Peamarsh turned from the table where she was kneading bread and asked, "Well, have you found him?" and he was shaking his head and about to answer when the bell rang. He saw her head go up as on the previous occasion, and the same expression came onto her face. Dusting her hands free of the flour, she said, "Who can this be?" She looked at Davy as she spoke, and he answered, "I don't know, miss. But should I go and see?"

"No, no, I'll go upstairs and see from the window." Then, about to turn away, she stopped, drew in a long breath and, nodding her head slowly, said, "Yes, yes, David; you go and see. Take the key." She pointed to the key hanging on the hook by the kitchen door. "It can't be anyone of importance." Then as John Willie made to follow Davy she held up her finger at him, indicating that he should stay, and Davy went out smiling.

She liked John Willie pottering about the kitchen. He carried her dirty dishes from the table to the sink. If cinders fell onto the hearth he swept them up with the tidy brush. Davy knew that he liked being with her as much as she liked having him. It was funny, he often thought, very funny that John Willie should have taken to her from the very first. And he was more free with her than he had been with his own mother. But then that wasn't his fault, for their mother had at times treated him with no more understanding than his father had done.

As he approached the gate he saw a man standing outside. It was no one he knew, at least so he thought until he actually reached the gate. And then he recognized Mr. Potter. He had never held Mr. Potter's horse; he had refused to join in the scramble for that honor. He saw immediately that Mr. Potter was amazed at the sight of him, and before he had managed to unlock the chain Mr. Potter was expressing his amazement.

"What are you doin' here? What's all this?" He stepped through the gate and confronted Davy.

"I work here."

"You what?"

"I said I work here." Davy's jaw was stiffening. He was finding he didn't like the man. He might be kind to Miss Peamarsh, but he still didn't like him.

Dan Potter was a short man, thick-set; he had a large nose with a wart on the side of it, and his head seemed to rest straight on his shoulders.

"Since when?"

"Oh, some time, weeks."

They were walking up the drive now, and Dan Potter paused in his step and screwed up his face as he said, "Weeks?"

"Aye, that's what I said, weeks." Davy looked at Dan Potter's red countenance. He was bristling like a turkey. What did it matter to him if he was working here or not? He should be glad that Miss Peamarsh had changed her ways and was having help.

Nothing more was said. They reached the back door, and as Davy was about to tap on it, as he always did on entering, the man, Potter, thrust it open and marched into the kitchen.

Davy saw immediately that Miss Peamarsh was startled. There was that look on her face again, the look she wore when she heard the bell ring.

"You!"

Miss Peamarsh cast a quick glance between Davy and John Willie; then, her eyes coming back to Dan Potter and her tone altering, she spoke more naturally, as one would expect of a mistress to an old servant. "I . . . I wasn't expecting you, Potter," she said.

"No, no, you weren't . . . miss, but . . . but I had a little business to transact this way so I thought I would look you up. I see you've taken on staff again?"

Davy saw Miss Peamarsh's back stiffen, while her head took on an angle that should have told anyone with sense to keep his place. But apparently Mr. Potter didn't know his place, judging by what he now said. "Very foolish thing to do if you ask me, miss. Very foolish."

"When I do ask you, that will be time enough for you to voice your opinion, Potter."

Again Miss Peamarsh cast a glance toward Davy and John Willie before turning abruptly, saying, "Kindly come into the study, Potter." And on this she went out of the kitchen and Dan Potter followed her. But not before he had given Davy a look that held not a little measure of vindictiveness.

The kitchen to themselves, Davy and John Willie instinctively drew together, and they both stood looking toward the door leading to the hall; then John Willie, looking up at Davy, said, "Huh! huh!"

The exclamation indicated an uneasiness, and

Davy, nodding down at him, muttered, "Aye, there's something fishy here." Potter was supposed to be kind to her, but it struck him that she was—he wouldn't even allow himself to think the word—frightened—for he couldn't imagine Miss Peamarsh being afraid of anything or anyone. Yet at the same time he knew he wasn't mistaken; she had been frightened by the sight of Potter, the man who had once been her servant.

Quickly now he indicated to John Willie that he stay where he was; then, tiptoeing toward the door that led into the hall, he opened it and thrust his head forward, listening. He could hear the murmur of voices but not what they were saying. He looked down at his feet. If he tried to go across the hall in his clogs the boards would squeak.

Bending down, he slipped them off, then with them in his hand he went into the hall.

He knew which was the door to the study, because that was the only room besides the attic he had been in since he had come here. Miss Peamarsh had had him move a desk in there because the moths had got into the carpet under it and eaten it bare.

Silently now he tiptoed toward the door. It was the second on the left and opposite the stairs. All the doors in the hall were deeply inset in the walls, and he stood within the first door while again poking his head forward. Then he almost jumped as Miss Peamarsh's voice came from the room, harsh and deep and using swear words. "Damn you, Dan Potter. Damn you! No, I say."

He was quite used to hearing swear words, but from ordinary people, not people like Miss Peamarsh, who was a parson's daughter.

Eeh! her, swearing. Miss Peamarsh, swearing.

Now Potter's voice came to him. In stiff, menacing

tones, he said, "I wouldn't be takin' that high-handed attitude if I was you, miss; we've gone along all this time all right, but now you're being silly."

"Don't you dare use that tone to me, or address me in that fashion. There are limits. Remember that, Potter; there are limits to what a person can stand. And I have thought more than once lately that I am paying too big a price for your silence."

"Well, I should think again, miss, if I was you. Eight years come January the memorial service was held in the chapel. Now you wouldn't like that to be forgotten, would you?"

"You're a fiend, Potter. That's what you are, a fiend. From the day my father brought you into this house as a boy I recognized you as a fiend, a sly, sneaking fiend."

"Be careful, miss, be careful." Dan Potter's voice no longer sounded smooth. "Anyway, what's a hundred pounds."

"I haven't got a hundred pounds; you know that quite well. You know what my income is, and you take two-thirds of it."

"Aye, aye, I know. An' it's very kind of you to part with it, an' I appreciate it . . . ."

"Stop that twaddle!" There followed a silence; then her voice again harsh, yet weary-sounding, "When you know what my income is, how do you expect me to have an extra hundred pounds to give you?"

"Well, miss, money doesn't lie just in coin; there are such things as valuables that can be turned into money. I was thinking of the miniatures that are lying useless in the cases in the drawing room. An' then there's your china. Two or three bits of that would bring a hundred or more, I dare say."

"Never! never!"

"Now, now, don't be too hasty, miss. Think . . . think carefully. I'll give you me word I won't ask it again, not for any extra, but at the moment I'm pushed for ready money. It's this bit of business I'm going into, as I've told you."

"Well, Potter, whatever business it is it will receive no help from me. You can make up your mind once and for all on that. And how dare you suggest I sell my possessions! You have gone too far, Potter, too far."

In the silence that followed, Davy was about to move back to the kitchen when he was riveted to the spot by the handle of the study door being wrenched open and Miss Peamarsh's voice saying one word, "Out!"

Instinctively his hand darted behind him and found the knob, and the next minute he had slipped into the room and was standing, scarcely breathing, with his back to the closed door.

He put his hand to his mouth now as Dan Potter's growling voice came almost, it would seem, into his ear, saying, "I think you're bein' foolish, miss, if you permit me to say so; for after all, I ask you, will you miss one or two trinkets out of that lot? An' who sees them anyway?"

"No! Once and for all, I say no. Do your worst; but remember, Potter, if you have a hold on me, I have one on you. You have blackmailed me for years, and blackmailing is a very serious offense; it could mean prison. And let me tell you that if ten years ago I had not been so afraid, so distressed, this situation would never have come about. You could have done your worst. And now I warn you, Potter, I am near the end of my rope, and I'm quite capable of letting justice take its course."

"Not you, miss, not you." Potter's voice sounded like a sneer now. "Just think of the family name. You've always been so proud of the family name, haven't you? An' the dear old vicar. Just think of the effect on the poor old vicar."

"Get out! Go this minute."

"Aye . . . I'll go, miss, an' give you time to think it over. An' you will think it over, I'm sure. But I'll be back. An' one more thing. What I said when I first came in I'll repeat. With those two out there you're takin' a risk, a big risk. I never thought you'd be that foolish. Take my advice an' send them packin'."

"When I want any advice from you at all, Potter, I'll ask you for it. And that day, as I can see, is a long way off. Now go."

Davy heard the kitchen door open, then close, then the back door open and bang. He waited to hear his name being called, because if she should ask for him John Willie might point toward the hall. Eeh! he didn't want her to find him here.

For the first time he turned and looked at the room. It was gloomy, for the curtains were drawn. But he could see that it was a big room and there were dust covers over most of the furniture. There were glass-fronted cabinets in two recesses standing against the far wall, and he saw immediately that the contents must be those that Potter had referred to, for they were full of odds and ends of china. There were pictures lining three of the walls, but the far wall was taken up with the window.

He made his way rapidly to the window now, but paused when he came opposite the fireplace and glanced up at a big portrait hanging there. It showed a man standing at the head of a horse. He was in riding clothes with shining leather gaiters. And there was something else that shone out of the picture into the dimness of the room. It came from a kind of scarf buckle at the man's neck. During his fleeting glance he thought that the man must be the parson, but by the time he had reached the window he had discarded this assumption, thinking it was too young for a parson; likely his son, Miss Peamarsh's brother.

He went behind the curtains and as quietly as he could he unlatched the window and raised it, then stepped outside and drew the window down again, telling himself as he did so that he must find a way to bolt the window from the inside again.

Getting into his clogs now, he hurried round to the back of the house, there to see Miss Peamarsh standing in the yard.

"Where have you been, boy? Go down to the gate. Let Mr. Potter out, then lock it. . . . Lock it."

He looked into her white face as he said, "Yes, miss. Yes, miss." Then he ran from her, only to stop. He had hung the key on the hook again. Now he dashed toward the kitchen, passing her without a word, grabbed the key up, then raced down the drive to find Potter standing at the gates.

The man's face looked almost purple, and he did not speak until he had passed through the gates, and then, pointing his finger toward Davy, he said, "If you've any sense, lad, you'll get out of here an' quick. You don't know what you've let yourself in for."

Davy made no reply. He just returned the man's ferocious stare and locked the gates, but he did not immediately go back up the drive. He took the bordered path to the side, and some way along it he stopped and, putting his hand to his chin, rubbed it slowly.

What had she done? It must have been something

big, pretty awful, when she was giving that bloke so much of her money. And whatever it was, it was the reason for her living as she did, and also—he now nodded his head at himself—for her pretending that she was a bit queer, for he had come to know she was no more queer than he himself was. Snappy, bossy at times, but not queer.

And there was another side to her that he hadn't seen in any other woman that he had known. This was very evident when she was dealing with John Willie. It was a soft, tender side, more than motherly even. . . . But what had she done? It must have been something that you could call criminal, else she wouldn't be paying Potter big money. And it must have been something that he had found out about her when he was living here. But what? Aye, what? Again he shook his head before moving slowly up the path and going across the yard and into the kitchen.

John Willie was alone, and immediately he ran to Davy and gave three rapid deep "Huhs." Then putting his hand to his head he slowly drew it over his brow and down his face, and Davy nodded at him in confirmation, for John Willie was telling him that the miss had a long, sad face.

John Willie now pointed toward the door. But Davy shook his head; he wouldn't dare go through there unless she called him.

He stood in the kitchen for about five minutes before he decided what to do. He had forgotten that the last thing he had been doing was looking for Snuffy; that was until the door opened again and Miss Peamarsh entered. And he was more than taken aback when, walking directly to the table and carrying on with her baking as if she had never left it, she said, "Well, did you find Rex?"

"Rex? Oh, no. No, miss."

She raised her head. "Why are you looking at me like that, boy?" Her tone was not as usual but slightly faltering, and his, too, faltered as he answered, "Just because . . . because I thought you didn't look too good, miss."

"I am perfectly good . . . perfectly well, I mean. . . . Don't stand there—go and find the animal."

"Yes, miss." He turned away and opened the door, then stopped and on a relieved laugh said, "He's here, miss. He's coming across the yard."

John Willie had also seen the dog, and he ran to him and caught hold of his rough and led him into the kitchen, and there he lowered his head and looked into Snuffy's face, as did Davy, for the dog's jaws were moving in a circular movement as if he were chewing something.

Bending down quickly, Davy pulled open the dog's mouth and eased from between its jaws a long piece of gristle, one end of which still bore traces of raw meat. He held it up and looked at Miss Peamarsh, saying, in a voice scarcely above a whisper, "It's . . . it's raw meat, miss. An' look, there's a bit of wool still on it. It's mutton . . . sheep."

Miss Peamarsh's hands had become still in the flour bowl, and they stared at each other. Then they both looked down on Snuffy, and the same thought was running through their minds. He was a sheep dog, and it wasn't unknown for a sheep dog to turn rogue if he was hungry. But then Snuffy had never gone hungry, not of late.

Miss Peamarsh now clapped her hands sharply over the bowl, then came toward Davy and looked more closely at the strip of gristle hanging from his fingers. And when she raised her eyes Davy said quickly, "No, no, miss, he's not, he'd never be a killer; he's as gentle as a lamb itself."

"How do you know? You don't know his pedigree. You said your father found him abandoned. Perhaps he wasn't abandoned without cause."

"We've had him for years, miss—seven or more."

"You may have, but instincts will out; sooner or later instincts will out. You know what this means, boy, you know the penalty for sheep stealing or sheep ravishing? Each sheep no longer claims a human life, but it could mean penal servitude if it was proved you were aware of his behavior. . . . As for him . . ."

"Miss, miss, he wouldn't. I'd stake me own life . . ."

"Don't make heroic speeches, boy; you just might have to, and within prison walls. This is serious. You realize this is very serious?"

They both turned and looked at the dog now, who was lying contentedly stretched out on the mat, with John Willie beside him. As usual John Willie had his arms around his neck, but his face wasn't buried in the dog's rough; it was turned up toward them, and their own apprehension was reflected in his eyes. He knew what all this was about.

"Well"—Miss Peamarsh drew in a long breath—"we'll just have to wait and see, won't we? In the meantime, take him to the woodshed and lock him in; he must be kept there until we see what happens. Now get on with your work."

Davy did as he was asked, but he had to pull John Willie away from the animal before he could shut the door of the woodshed, and when John Willie began huhing loudly, Davy turned on him, crying below his breath, "Shut up! Shut up, do you hear? As she said, there might be more than him polished off. . . . Do you understand that, eh? Do you understand?"

He didn't wait to see whether John Willie understood him or not but stalked away. With one thing and another that day he didn't know which way was up.

It was as his ma used to say: when life appeared too good to be true, look out.

Six

The rest of the day passed and nothing happened, and as Davy lay awake staring up at the rafters of the ceiling he reasoned that if a sheep had been bothered there would have been someone along before now, because Farmer Millbank would have searched out everybody who owned a dog.

And when the next morning the quiet of the house still was undisturbed and the routine went on as usual, he knew a measure of relief; that was until around two o'clock in the afternoon, when the bell rang again.

Startled by its clanging, he stood for a moment, his spade poised some inches above the soil. Then, throwing it down, he raced toward the yard, there to see Miss Peamarsh already crossing it. She stopped and waited for his coming. Then, her voice just above a whisper as if she might be heard as far away as the gate, she said, "Go into the kitchen, boy, and stay there. . . . Where is your brother?"

"In the woodshed with the dog." He found it difficult to call Snuffy "Rex."

"Well, bring him into the house and keep him there. And know this. If they have traced the killing to the animal I . . . I won't be able to help you. They will shoot him, make no bones about that. And what is more, you'll be held responsible." Her hand came out toward him but didn't touch him. Then, her tone sharp again, she said, "Go along now; do as I bid you," and she turned from him and went toward the gate.

He had to pull John Willie away from Snuffy, and when he banged the door on the dog and Snuffy barked he screwed up his eyes tightly for a moment. Then, gripping John Willie by the hand, he dragged him into the kitchen and pushed him onto a chair and with a stab of his finger indicated that he stay there and not move; then he went to the kitchen window and stood looking out, waiting.

It was almost ten minutes later when Miss Peamarsh returned, and she wasn't alone, but at the sight of the man accompanying her, Davy thrust his face close against the windowpane, his eyes squinting. He couldn't believe it. It wasn't Farmer Millbank, nor the sheriff, nor the Justice, nor even Potter; it was the redheaded man. He almost sprang to the door and pulled it open, and when Miss Peamarsh entered and the man followed her he gaped from the one to the other.

"Hello, lad."

"Hello." Davy could hardly hear his own voice.

Miss Peamarsh had walked toward the fire. There she turned, and, her back to it, she looked at Davy and said, "This is a Mr. Talbot; he says he's an acquaintance of yours."

"Aye, miss. Aye, he is." Davy glanced at the man,

and the man grinned at him. It was a merry, unself-conscious grin.

"He has something very interesting to impart. Perhaps you'd be good enough to tell the boy what you have told me, Mr. Talbot."

Davy saw that Miss Peamarsh, although not on her high horse, was nevertheless using her best manner. He also noted that it did not seem to have an intimidating effect on his redheaded friend, for although he had taken his cap off, his manner was in no way—what was the word? Miss Peamarsh would have known—well, his manner was not that of a workman or a servant; although his voice was different from hers, it was as if he were speaking to an equal. And then he said the most surprising thing. "As I just told the young lady here," he said—*young lady*. Fancy anyone calling Miss Peamarsh a young lady. Granted she wasn't old, but a young lady! Then he went on, "I explained that I was living temporarily in your old abode in the mine, and had got as far as the wall of her garden searching for brushwood to stock up for my fire when I heard this gnawing noise, a crunching sound like a fox finishing off a rabbit, you know. So, I investigated." He used words, Davy thought, almost as good as Miss Peamarsh. "And there I saw a dog gnawing away at the stump end of what must have been part of a leg of mutton. I'm sure you will understand, lad, as I haven't tasted meat for many a day, not even rabbit, I was hard put not to challenge the dog for what remained. Anyway, I realized I'd seen the beast afore. It was on the day I'd had a word with you when you were cleaning the gates, remember?"

Davy nodded; then the man went on, "And you remember what I said when you did me a kindness that few of your age would ever think about? I said I hoped to be able to pay you back in some way. Well, the dog and that piece of fresh meat intrigued me, so for the next few days I kept a lookout." He turned now and cast his glance toward Miss Peamarsh. "Having nothing better to do, it passed the time. And on the second day I was rewarded for my efforts." He nodded toward Davy now. "A lad came slinking round the corner, a pit lad. He had something under his coat. He crawled in under the brushwood, and when he came out the bulge had gone. I had a good look at him and knew I'd recognize him again, for I'd seen him once or twice afore.

"Well, I made my way in, and there, placed near a hole in the wall, was another shive of mutton, the wool still sticking to it. Can you imagine the temptation that was, lad?" He now bent his head toward Davy. "The saliva dribbled down my chin." He laughed, then glanced again toward Miss Peamarsh, who was staring at him, her face straight, and he nodded at her now, saying, "Although my life's been pretty rough of late, miss, I still value it, so my good sense got the better of my need and I left the meat there and waited. Sure enough, through the hole along came our friend the sheep dog, and I watched him enjoy another marvelous meal.

"Yes, you may well look astonished, lad. Anyway, I did a little more investigating, and I found out the name of the kind lad who was supplying your dog with such luscious food, after which I traveled a few miles and had a talk here and there with farm workers, killing two birds with one stone, you might say. Well, what I learned was, there were no jobs to be had; and also there was a tale going round that a dog had been seen ravishing a sheep. Somebody had told somebody who had told somebody, but as yet the carcass hadn't been found. So, as one old codger said, no carcass no proof, and it would take some dog to finish off a sheep without leaving any trace at all. All the talk was just for something to say. But now"—he nodded at Davy—"I think in a very short while the remains of the carcass will be found just outside the hole in the wall. How they'll prove that the animal dragged it there God alone knows. It's my belief that they'll try to prove that it was carried there some time ago by a hungry lad who had his young brother to care for, that was before this lady"—he inclined his head toward Miss Peamarsh—"took him into her service. When the search party is led through the thicket, they'll find quite a number of half-chewed bones and lots of hair, hair and skin, for no dog's going to bother himself with bones if he can get flesh meat, even if it's stinking. So that's the picture, lad. . . . I'd like to ask you one question. What have you ever done to the Coxons to make them so vindictive that they'd put your liberty at stake? An' not so long ago it could've been your life that was at stake. Do you know that?"

All of a sudden Davy felt faint. Even in the pit disaster, struggling against being drowned in the black swirling water, he hadn't felt like this. The weight of the man's words were pressing him down: "What have you ever done to the Coxon boys to make them so vindictive that they'd put your liberty at stake?"

"Sit down, sit down, lad." The man was pressing him into a chair. Davy blinked his eyes, gulped, shook his head, then looked to where Miss Peamarsh was standing in front of him, and he almost whimpered, "I, I could be sent along the line . . . I mean put in prison. . . . John Willie. . . ."

"Don't worry. Don't worry." Miss Peamarsh's face was close to his. It didn't seem like her face at this moment; her eyes were brown and soft, her skin was flushed, her mouth was slightly open. For a fraction of a second she represented the man's description of a young woman. She moved away from him, then came back within a moment, saying, "Drink this. Drink it all up."

He drank from the cup. He didn't know what it was, only that it was something in hot water that stung his throat.

Miss Peamarsh was now patting John Willie on the head and bending over him, saying, "He's all right. He's all right." Then, straightening up, she looked at the visitor and said, "What do you suggest we do, Mr. . . . Mr. Talbot?"

"Well, miss, since you ask me, I would suggest that we, I mean the lad and meself, keep watch until the culprit shows up again. Then we'll nab him and bring him in here. And if I was in your place, miss, I would send for his father, because that lad hasn't worked out a thing like this on his own, an' I'd have somebody here of authority to meet the man. If you want to take the matter to the Justices, well, then I'd have a Justice here, although you know what that could mean, miss. As the boy here has said, you can be put along the line for sheep stealing or be deported, so, if you didn't want to go that far, perhaps the parson or someone of a forgiving nature would be best, but someone who at the same time carries authority. That's what I would do, but of course it's in your hands, miss."

Miss Peamarsh blinked rapidly as she looked at the tall thin man; and then she turned away from him before she spoke, saying, "Yes, yes, I think you're right, Mr. Talbot. And I think you should begin at once; there's no time like the present." She now looked at Davy, and as he rose to his feet she said, "Do you feel well enough?"

"Aye . . . yes, miss, I'm . . . I'm all right."

"Well then, go along with this"—for a moment Davy thought she was going to say gentleman, then she changed it to—"with Mr. Talbot. But first you must take something to eat with you. Wait a moment."

Now both Peter Talbot and Davy watched her buttering thick slices of bread and placing large cuts of cheese on them. When she had made six sandwiches she put them into a clean napkin and handed them to Davy, saying, "This will keep you going until later. And . . . and here, you'll want something to drink." She stretched out her hand and lifted a can of milk from the delf rack. This she handed to Peter Talbot, and he, taking it from her, looked at her for a moment before saying, "Thank you. Thank you, miss, most warmly." Then they both turned and went out, while she held onto John Willie's hand to stop him from following them.

There was no meat outside the hole, but Davy was amazed to see, as Peter Talbot had described, a number of gnawed bones and pieces of sheepskin with hair still attached to them. He shuddered as he looked at them, for he knew what their discovery could have meant to himself, and once more he became weighed down with fear.

Peter Talbot, now putting his fingers to his lips, indicated caution, then led Davy through a narrow opening that he had made in the bramble along by the wall, and from there they doubled back on their tracks to a spot where the brambles and bracken were beaten down and which overlooked the clearing in front of the hole in the wall.

"Squat down here and you'll be able to see through the thicket," Peter said to Davy.

When Davy got down onto his hands and knees he saw that they were within a foot of the little clearing he himself had made to get to the hole in the wall and where now the bones were scattered.

When Peter was sitting beside him he said softly, "I wouldn't mind starting on one of those sandwiches, if you've got no objections, lad."

"Oh, aye. Aye. Have the lot," Davy whispered, then thrust the bundle of food into Peter's hands, and he again experienced a feeling of guilt as he watched him gulp down two of the cheese sandwiches almost in seconds.

After the first hour of waiting, the time hung heavy; with every scuttle in the undergrowth they became still. It wasn't until the afternoon light had almost gone and they were going to give up for the day that they both stiffened into alertness at the sound that was most certainly not made by the scurrying of an animal.

Exchanging quick glances, they peered through the thicket, and they saw him . . . Fred Coxon. He was in his pit clothes, and they watched him draw from under his short jacket a piece of meat, faint pink on one side with flesh, gray on the other with wool. They watched him bend down and place it on the ground before the hole. And it was as he straightened his back that he let out a scream like that of a trapped animal, for Peter Talbot's sinewy arm had thrust itself through the bramble and caught him by the collar.

What happened next was painful for the three of them, especially for Davy, as he went through the brambles face first and threw himself on the struggling figure and, locked together, they rolled over the bones until Peter dragged Davy from the boy. Then he stood over Fred Coxon, where he lay now on his back staring upward with a petrified look on his face.

"Come on, you, to your feet." Gripping Coxon's shoulder, Peter yanked him upward, only immediately to push him downward again toward the hole. Then, taking his foot, he thrust it into his buttocks, saying, "Get yourself through, you," and turning to Davy he asked, "Are you all right, lad?"

Davy could only nod. There was blood running into his mouth from the scratches on his face, but he was oblivious to the pain, for he was filled with the desire to knock the stuffing out of that sneaking malicious weasel.

It was Peter who held onto young Coxon and thrust him through the tangled orchard and across the rough lawn, over the yard, to the back door, and then into the kitchen.

Miss Peamarsh turned startled from the fireplace when the three entered the room. Then, drawing herself to her full height, she looked down on the bowed head of Fred Coxon and said, "So this is he, is it, the sheep stealer?"

"I didn't. I didn't."

For answer to this, Davy pushed the freshly cut piece of mutton almost into his face, and Fred Coxon cringed back from it as if it were alive.

"What have you to say for yourself?"

Coxon's head was still down as he muttered, "Nowt. I'm sayin' nowt."

"We'll see about that," Miss Peamarsh said, and looking at Peter Talbot she went on, "It is up to us now to carry out your suggestion, Mr. Talbot. So, David"—she turned to Davy—"go as quickly as you

can to the vicarage and ask Parson Murray if he'd be
kind enough to come here. Tell him the urgency of
the situation. But . . . but before you go"—she moved
a step nearer to him—"wash your face. I will give you
some goose fat for the scratches when you return."

Davy said no word; he just nodded once, then
turned about and went swiftly out. But before he had
gone half across the yard Miss Peamarsh's voice
brought him to a halt and back to her side. "It will
soon be dark," she said; "you had better take a lantern." Then, her voice dropping, she added, "Tell the
parson all that has transpired, and ask him on my
behalf if it would be wise for you to go and bring the
boy's father tonight, or would it be preferable to let
him stew in his own juice, so to speak, and send for
him in the morning?"

Parson Murray was astounded by Davy's tale and
immediately was put into a quandary by the enormity
of the crime. He knew that were he to do his duty he
should contact the Justice and get him to accompany
him back to the Manor. But what would that mean?
Prison or deportation? What would Christ have done?
It was all very difficult. But one thing he did not agree
with was letting the father of the boy stew in any juice,
as Miss Peamarsh had suggested, and so it was a very
surprised Mr. Coxon who opened the door to Davy
and saw in the light of the lantern the parson sitting
in his gig.

"What's this? What's this?"

Before Davy could make any reply Parson Murray
called out, "You will be wise, Mr. Coxon, to accompany me to the Manor, where at this moment your son
is being held, having been found, I understand, placing cuts from a sheep as bait for a dog."

"What . . . what d'ya mean?"

"You know what I mean, Mr. Coxon; I'm sure your son has not accomplished this feat on his own. Now, are you going to accompany me, or have I to go on to the Justice and get him to visit you?"

Matthew Coxon turned and looked at his wife, who had come to his side, and the children who were swarming about him, and when she cried, "Eeh! I told you. I told you," he barked at her, "Shut up! Damn you, woman, shut up!" Then pushing her and the children back into the room, he grabbed up his coat and cap and with a slow stride came toward the gig. But as he went to mount, the parson checked him with, "There's only room for two, as you can see. You will be obliged to walk."

The oath that Matthew Coxon brought out also brought forth censure from the parson. "That language won't help you any, Mr. Coxon. And remember that. Come up, Davy." He motioned Davy up to his side; then, whipping up the horse, they went off at a trot.

It was Miss Peamarsh herself who opened the gates. Holding the lantern high, she looked at Parson Murray and said, "I am sorry to trouble you, Parson," and he answered, "That is quite all right, Miss Peamarsh. Would you mind leaving the gate open? The man, Coxon, is following. Davy here can wait for him."

"No, no, I'll wait. Go on up to the house, please."

Her tone was such that the parson did not argue with her but whipped up the horse again.

Miss Peamarsh waited at the open gate until she saw the hurrying figure of Matthew Coxon, and when he came abreast of her he glared at her, but she smiled at him and said strange words: "The mills of God grind slow, Mr. Coxon, but they are known to grind exceeding small."

"Blast you!"

Miss Peamarsh said nothing to this but closed the gates, locked them, then walked on ahead of her latest visitor.

Davy thought that that kitchen had never known so many people all at once for many a year, nor seen so strange an assembly, nor yet listened to such cross-talk. He had never been in a Court of Justice in his life, but he felt that the kitchen had taken on the air of such a place, with Mr. Coxon protesting loudly, at first that was, that he would have them all up for taking his character away, he would that, while at the same time prompting his son what to say and what not to say. Then there were the quiet, measured tones of Parson Murray and the stringent interjections of Peter Talbot. The only people other than himself who hadn't opened their mouths to speak so far were Miss Peamarsh and, of course, their John Willie.

But now Miss Peamarsh cut off another tirade of Matthew Coxon's by exclaiming sharply, "Be quiet! Let us have no more of this. You are guilty of stealing a sheep, but your guilt is trebled in my opinion by your using the animal to incriminate an innocent person, knowing what the penalty of such an act is. And you do know that, Matthew Coxon, don't you; you know what the penalty is for stealing a sheep? Yet you have harbored so much spite against the boy here"—she indicated Davy without looking at him—"that you resort to this diabolical plan to lay the blame on him. Now we will have no more talk. You will either own up to the crime and sign a paper that Parson Murray will write out, or tomorrow morning you will find yourself taken into custody. You have your choice.

Now!" She raised her hand swiftly. "I said we will have no more of your protestations. You will say yes, or no."

There was silence in the kitchen. All eyes were on Matthew Coxon, whose face, from being red with his blustering, now looked a dirty gray, but he didn't speak. It was Fred Coxon who broke the silence. Gripping his father's arm, he cried, "Da! Da! Go on, man, tell them. You'll have to."

"Shut up, you!" Matthew Coxon's voice was a growl, yet now his head was bent until his chin almost rested on his chest, and his voice came as a thick mutter as he said, "I didn't steal it, an' I didn't kill it; I found it mauled. It . . . it was rotten."

"No, no; the pieces of meat I saw weren't rotten."

Matthew Coxon was now glaring up under his lids at Peter, and the two men outstared each other in the lamplight for a moment before Coxon spluttered, "It was. It was, I tell you. It was rotten."

"Well now, well now, rotten or fresh"—the minister was speaking now—"you admit to cutting up the animal with the intent, as Miss Peamarsh has stated, of putting the blame onto this boy, knowing the terrible results that could have followed. And I may state at this moment that you would have great difficulty in proving that the animal was rotten when you found it. Farmer Millbank is not the man to leave a rotten carcass lying around, and I presume the animal to be his. . . . Well, having got this far, it remains to be seen what action is to be taken against you, and in justice I think this should be the decision of one person: the boy here. You will pardon me saying so, Miss Peamarsh"—the minister now turned his head toward Miss Peamarsh—"I think it only fair that we leave it to him whether the Justice be called or whether a more lenient view be taken. Now, boy, say your piece."

Davy's eyes moved around the group of people at the table until they met those of Matthew Coxon, and he experienced a human spurt of triumph as he read the fear in their depths. He had but to say the word and Coxon and his Fred could go along the line, the line that led to deportation and Australia, if nothing worse.

Before dragging his eyes away, he watched the beads of sweat roll slowly down from the man's brow onto his broad nose and gather in a heavy drop at the end. He looked toward the woman who had taken him and John Willie into her life, and he said quietly, "Let it be as Miss Peamarsh said. But I'd ask one thing to be added to the paper, that if he tries to harm me or mine anymore, then the matter of the sheep will be brought into the open."

As Miss Peamarsh moved her head once in his direction, the minister let out a long sigh, after which he said, "Would you oblige me, Miss Peamarsh, with some writing materials?"

There was a strained, embarrassed silence in the kitchen while Miss Peamarsh was out and it was only broken by her entry again.

All their eyes were now directed toward the minister where he sat writing on a sheet of paper, and what he had to say filled one side and halfway down the other. When it was finished he read it aloud, and what he had written covered the whole situation. Then, pushing the paper slowly across the table, he said briefly, "Your mark, Coxon. Place it next to your name there." He put his finger on the paper and waited while Matthew Coxon's shaking hand took the pen and made a cross. "And now you."

"He doesn't need to sign anything."

"Oh, but he does." The parson brought his head

down in a grave movement. "He is your son and he was more than a party to this act. Put your cross there, boy."

Without hesitation Fred Coxon made his cross. And now the parson said, "And you, Mr. Talbot. What is your Christian name?"

"Peter."

As the parson went to write the name, Peter put in sharply, "I can write my own signature, sir."

"Oh. Oh, very good." The parson now looked toward Peter with interest, and, seeming to forget the seriousness of the occasion, he smiled and said, "Can you read also?"

"Yes, I can read also." Peter's voice was flat and his face was straight as he looked at the parson, and the parson, now slightly flustered, muttered, "Oh. Oh, that's good."

"And now you, Miss Peamarsh."

Firmly Miss Peamarsh wrote her name in bold letters under the others; and lastly the parson signed the paper, and when it was done he folded up the sheet. Then, looking toward where Matthew Coxon was sitting with his hands gripped tightly in front of him, he said, "I will make three copies of this. One I shall give to the boy, one will be in Miss Peamarsh's keeping, and one I shall hold myself. I am telling you this, Coxon, in case it enters your head to try to regain this paper and destroy it. Now I'd advise you to take your leave, and as quickly as possible. And remember what the boy here said. Should you in any way try to harm him, or his, this matter will come into the open and you will suffer the consequences then, as you would now but for his leniency. Go, get yourself away, man."

Matthew Coxon was the last to rise from the table. He seemed to have to hold onto it for support. After looking from one to the other as if he could murder them all on the spot, he turned slowly about and stumped out of the room to join his son, who had already scampered into the yard.

The parson now shook Miss Peamarsh by the hand and said his farewells to her; then, turning to Davy, he said, "You are a very lucky boy, Davy. This night might have been a tragic one for you."

"It would that, sir, if it hadn't been for Mr. Talbot here."

The minister now turned to Peter and said, "Yes, yes, of course." Then, his tone slightly condescending, he said, "I was interested to hear that you can read and write."

"Were you, sir?"

"Yes." The syllable was hesitant.

"It may surprise you, sir, that many miners can read and write; times are changing and changing fast."

"Yes. Er, yes." The minister was definitely embarrassed; and now he turned again to Miss Peamarsh and said, "Good-night to you."

She accompanied him to the door, that was, after casting a probing glance at the man who had talked to the minister as if he were his equal.

When they had the kitchen to themselves Peter Talbot said, with some bitterness in his tone, "Can I read and write! Some of them don't hold with the ordinary man learning, you know, lad. Some parsons are for helping you along, but not all."

"Parson Murray's all right. He's kind."

"There's kindness and kindness, lad. . . . Anyway, the main thing is, it's over, and it's been like a bit out of a story book, hasn't it?"

"Aye, you could say it has. But . . . but I'm still shaking inside thinkin' of how the story might have turned out. Eeh! if you hadn't twigged, Peter. Eeh! it makes me shiver to think."

"Well, you'll have no more trouble from that quarter. You can rest assured on that."

"I hope not."

"Never fear; this night's been a lesson to them both they'll remember till their dying day. . . . Well now, lad, I'll be off an' all. I've got to put me house in order afore I can go to bed." He gave a slight laugh, and Davy, going to him, now whispered, "I'll ask her if you can sleep here. . . . "

He hadn't finished speaking when the door opened and Miss Peamarsh entered, and Davy, about to turn to her and make his request, was haltered by Peter's saying, "No, lad, no. Thanks all the same, but I'll be on my way."

"Were you refusing to have something to eat, Mr. Talbot?"

"No, ma'am, I never refuse anything to eat. I was simply refusing Davy's offer, through your permission that is, to bunk . . . to sleep the night in his rooms."

Miss Peamarsh looked from Peter to Davy now, then down to John Willie, who was standing close to him, and she blinked as she usually did when slightly uncertain of the attitude she should adopt. Looking back at Peter now, she said, "You're welcome to stay with the boy for tonight if you so wish."

"Thank you, miss. I appreciate your kindness, but if it's all the same to you I'll make for the mine."

"The mine?"

"Yes, I've taken over young Davy's apartment there. It isn't too uncomfortable; I've been in many worse. Now I'll say good-night to you. . . . "

"Wait. Wait. You . . . you must take some food with you and . . . and a hot drink. Wait; sit down a moment." She pointed imperiously to a chair, and with a half-smile at Davy, he did as he was told.

They watched her pack up more cheese sandwiches, and when she took some eggs from a dish and turned her head in Peter's direction, saying, "You have a pan?" he nodded at her and answered, "Yes, I have a pan."

When a few minutes later she handed him the bundle of food, he looked from it to her and spoke softly, saying, " 'And the Samaritan took him to an inn and said, Look after him, and whatever I owe you I'll pay you on my return.' I always like to pay my debts, ma'am. I've paid one the night." He cast a glance in Davy's direction, then ended, "I may be able to do something for you an' all someday."

Davy watched Miss Peamarsh swallow twice before saying, "I'm glad to hear you know your Bible, Mr. Talbot."

"I was brought up on it, miss. Good-night to you now, and thank you again." He turned from her and looked toward Davy. Then putting his hand out he gripped his shoulder. "Be seeing you, lad. An' you an' all, young 'un." He now flicked John Willie's chin with his finger.

Davy said nothing by way of farewell. He was filled with a number of strange sensations, all mixed up with his new friend and Miss Peamarsh and the events of this day.

When the door closed on Peter Talbot, Miss Peamarsh stood for a long moment without moving; then she turned to Davy and said abruptly, "Well, that's enough excitement for one day. Have something to eat, then get yourself to bed, both of you."

As she marched out of the kitchen Davy and John Willie looked at each other, and John Willie gave a small "Huh" while Davy thought, Trust her to bring things down to brass tacks. The expression didn't fit exactly what he meant; he only knew that of a sudden everything had gone flat.

He felt very tired. He took a slice of bread from the table, buttered it and handed it to John Willie; then indicating that he should follow him he went out and across the yard and up the stairs and into the rooms he thought of now as . . . his house. But tonight he did not set a match to the fire as was usual and sit by it with John Willie and look at the picture books Miss Peamarsh had given him; instead after lighting the lamp he undressed immediately. John Willie did the same, and without question, and together they got into bed. When John Willie snuggled up to him he put his arm about him and held him close until he went to sleep.

Although he was very tired, he himself could not go to sleep, and for a long time his thoughts centered about the narrow escape he'd had.

It wasn't until he was on the point of sleep that his mind touched on the events of yesterday. He had almost forgotten about Dan Potter, and thinking of him led naturally to Miss Peamarsh. And now he became wide awake again. Vividly he saw the scene around the kitchen table earlier this evening when he had imagined it was like a Court of Justice. He became slightly sick now at the thought that it might have been Miss Peamarsh sitting in Matthew Coxon's chair and being judged. But for what? Aye, that was it, for what?

Seven

It wasn't long before Davy found out "for what."

For four whole days things seemed to have gone back to normal, and Miss Peamarsh appeared to be her usual self. John Willie followed her about and she liked it, while Davy himself continued with the work of clearing the kitchen garden. The only one who didn't seem to want life to go on as usual was Snuffy.

Whenever possible Snuffy made for the hole in the wall even when he knew he couldn't get through, for Davy had blocked it up with the fallen stones, shoring them into place with planks of wood. But with the memory of his mutton feasts still in his mind, Snuffy roamed the tangled orchard, looking for a way out.

It was Saturday, and Miss Peamarsh always allowed Davy to stop work early on a Saturday.

After cleaning his tools and putting them away he went to the kitchen to collect John Willie and to clean him up for tea. But John Willie wasn't there; Miss Peamarsh said he had gone out to look for Rex, so he went looking for both John Willie and Snuffy.

It was no use calling, although now and again he whistled, hoping that the dog would hear him and this would bring John Willie running too.

He went around the outhouses and the tumbledown greenhouses, then across to the meadow, and lastly to that part of the garden where the old summerhouse was.

It was as he neared the summerhouse that he met John Willie head on. The boy's eyes were wide and he grabbed at his hands while spluttering a rapid succession of huhs.

"What is it? What's the matter?"

"Huh. Huh. Huh."

Davy allowed himself to be tugged behind the summerhouse and through the thicket to where there was a clearing of sorts, owing to the brambles having been scraped up. And there he stopped to stare down in horror at Snuffy, who, half hidden underneath two planks of wood, was scattering earth right and left from around, of all things, a human skeleton.

He stared unbelieving at the ribs sticking through the soil, while fully exposed lay the bones of an arm, and at the top of the arm, as if the thing lying there had turned its head toward its shoulder in deep thought or shame, rested a lower jawbone.

Now almost springing on Snuffy, he dragged the dog from the grave, for that's what it was, a grave; but no ordinary grave, for the body could not have been buried more than two feet or so below the level of the ground.

As he crouched over Snuffy, who stood gasping, his tongue lolling as if he had been enjoying a fine game, he knew a moment of lightning illumination, and he jerked his head to look at John Willie, expecting in a way to find on his face confirmation of his thoughts. But what he saw on John Willie's face was a reflection of his own showing open horror, and something more, fear. And he was forced to say while demonstrating with one hand, "It's all right. It's all right." Then, pushing Snuffy toward John Willie, he ended, "Here, hold him."

His head bobbing unconsciously on his shoulders, he gazed down on the partly exposed skeleton. He . . . he would have to cover it up. But . . . but he couldn't; he hadn't a shovel. Well, he couldn't leave it like this, could he? He must use his hands.

Kneeling down, he half closed his eyes and was on the point of turning his head away as he attempted to rake the soil over the skeleton when something bright caught his eye. It was lying just below the chin. He stared at it. He knew he had seen that before, or something like it. A buckle or a ring. Aye, it was like a muffler ring. And he remembered where he had seen it. Although it had been but a flashing glimpse, it was the red stone in the center of the tie ring which had, on that day when he was in the drawing room, cast a dull gleam down into the darkened room. And now here it was again, half covered with dirt but still gleaming.

His hands became still in the soil. No, no, it couldn't be. . . . But, aye, it was. The man lying there was the man in the picture over the fireplace in the unused drawing room. Eeh! this is what it was all about; this was why Dan Potter had a hold over her. This . . . this thing here was the man who was supposed to have gone to foreign parts.

He wanted to be sick. When his stomach heaved he

swallowed deeply. Then with frantic movements, not unlike those with which Snuffy had exposed the corpse, he began to cover it, but not to the same depth as it was before, for the earth was scattered too widely.

When the bones were no longer visible he pulled the two planks farther forward to help cover the loose soil. Then going to where John Willie was holding onto the dog he dropped on to his hunkers, and now slowly and solemnly he placed his fingers on his own lips and patted them three times; then pointing to the grave he shook his head slowly from side to side.

Staring widely at him, John Willie emitted a faint "Huh," after which Davy nodded at him, then waited for the nod to be returned. And when John Willie's head bobbed twice he said, "Good. . . . Come on." And on this he took his brother's hand and hurried him and the dog away from the scene.

But once clear of the orchard, he stopped and stood looking down on Snuffy. There was one thing certain: the dog couldn't be allowed to roam, for he'd make straight for the grave again. He'd have to lock him in the woodshed. Yet what excuse could he give to her for keeping Snuffy locked up? He looked up into the fading light and muttered aloud, "Eeh! to think she could do that. And to her brother!" He couldn't take it in.

He recalled faintly that young Master Richard Peamarsh had been known as a bit of a lad, a bit wild, but likable all the same, as the parson, his father, was. Oh yes, his father had been liked; people still talked about Parson Peamarsh as being a good man in all ways.

No. No. She couldn't have done that.

Well, why was she giving Dan Potter nearly all her money, and seemingly had done so for years?

He walked slowly on. How was he going to face her

now knowing what he knew about her? She had committed one murder; what if she tried it again? She had
a temper. Eeh! What was he thinking? She almost
loved John Willie here; as for himself, he thought she
liked him too. And what was more, he knew that no
matter how high-handed and independent she acted
at times, she was lonely. Aye, when he came to think
of it, he had never met anybody so lonely as her. And
so, he couldn't just scoot off and leave her. It was as
if he were answering himself and that "scooting off"
had been his intention. And it had been for a moment.
. . . Yet how was he going to face her and act ordinary
like? Well, he would soon know.

They went over the lawns and through the yard and
straight to the wood house where he locked Snuffy in;
then, after he had washed his hands and face
thoroughly under the pump and made John Willie do
the same, they went upstairs to change their jackets.

Ten minutes later they entered the kitchen.

"You've found him then? I saw you putting him in
the woodshed. Where was he?"

He was looking into her face. It was, he thought for
the first time, a nice face, a kind face. Yet she had done
that. It came to him that it was odd the things he was
finding out about her all at once.

"What is it, boy? What's the matter?"

"N . . . nothin', miss. Nothin'."

"Why are you looking at me like that?"

"Was I, miss? Oh, it was likely that I hadn't seen you
in that frock afore."

She looked down at her dress. "I've worn this all
day, and yesterday too."

"Have you, miss?" He gave a shaky laugh. "That's
me; me ma always used to say I never had me eyes
open until it was time to go to bed again." Again the
shaky laugh.

She stared at him in silence for a moment, then said, "I asked you where you found him."

"Beyond the paddock, miss."

"What was he doing there?"

He almost blurted out, "Scratching up bones," but he gulped on it and answered, "There's some rabbit burrows there; he . . . he's got the taste of meat, you see, after . . . after the sheep business, miss."

"Oh yes, yes." She nodded her head; then turning to the table she said, "It's Sunday tomorrow, your leave time; are you going to see your friend?"

. . . "Aye. Aye, I was, miss."

"Well then, you must take him some food and some milk."

"Thanks, miss, thanks."

"He must find it very unpleasant sleeping in the mine."

"Oh, I don't know, miss. No place is too bad as long as it's dry like. You get used to the floor."

She turned and looked at him, and her expression yet once again had changed. There was a softness on her face and in her voice as she said, "Yes, of course; you've had experience of it." Then, looking at John Willie, she beckoned him to her, and when he unhesitatingly went to her side she took his hand but addressed her remarks to Davy, saying, "I was going to measure him. There are lots of clothes packed away upstairs, shirts and trousers and such things. I can remake them. All but the coats." She gave a shy smile at this point, then added, "And for you, too, of course."

"Thank you, miss."

. . . "David"—they were facing each other now, quite close—"is anything wrong?"

. . ."No, no, miss."

"Are you sure?"

"Yes, miss. Only . . . well, I've felt a bit off the day."

"Ill?"

"No, not exactly, miss. I . . . I think it's because of the do the other day and thinkin' what . . . well, what could have happened to me."

"Oh yes, yes, I understand. It is a sort of delayed reaction to the event. Yes, yes, I understand. Sit down; I will give you some cordial and we won't have any lesson tonight. Then you must get to bed early, and tomorrow you must take the whole day off, and if it's fine, go walking and see your old friends. You have mentioned Mr. Cartwright in the village; you must visit him. I . . . I remember Mr. and Mrs. Cartwright." She nodded her head.

"Yes, yes, miss. Yes, I will."

"Good. Now I'll go and bring some of these things down, and after you've eaten we'll take some measurements."

She seemed to hover over him for a moment, her face so soft, her eyes so kind that he had to lower his gaze from hers.

When she had gone from the room he still sat with his head bowed, and now he asked himself the straight question, Could she have murdered somebody?

And the only answer he got was, Well, if she hadn't, why was she paying money to a blackmailer? And why had she locked up the whole place and made herself into an oddity just to keep people out?

Eight

They were sitting some way back in the mine, Davy, John Willie and Peter Talbot, and Peter now was staring at Davy with a look of disbelief on his face.

"You're not making this up, lad?"

"Aw"—Davy tossed his head almost angrily—"why would I make up a thing like that?"

"Aye, why would you make up a thing like that? But at the same time I can't take it in. Are you sure the ring you saw in the ground was the same as you saw in the picture?"

"Aye, aye, I'm sure, 'cos I sneaked in this morning when she was over milkin' the cow and there it was. The fellow in the picture was wearin' it."

"And you say she pays this Potter man two-thirds of her money?"

"That's what I heard."

"My God!" Peter was now rubbing his hand all round his unshaven face, and the sound was like the rasping of sandpaper.

"I . . . I had to tell somebody." There was an apologetic note in Davy's voice, and Peter said, "Aye, lad, aye, of course, you had. You couldn't carry a thing like that on your shoulders. And as you've just said, if Snuffy gets out on his own again he'll make straight for there." He put out his hand and patted the dog's head. "There's only one consolation: you say she never goes that way at all."

"No, no, she doesn't, but"—and now Davy rubbed his hand all round his face—"I had a nightmare last night an' I saw Snuffy landin' in the kitchen with an arm bone."

"And your nightmare could easily become a day-mare, couldn't it?"

They nodded at each other.

Peter now rose to his feet and went to the mouth of the mine and stood looking out, and he muttered, more to himself than to Davy, "People's lives. The things they hide, the burdens they carry. Life, what's it for, anyway?"

Davy came slowly to his side now and looked straight ahead too as he said, "What am I to do?"

"That's a question, lad, I can't answer at the moment. But there's one thing puzzlin' me. Why had it to be the dog that unearthed him? He must have been lying there a long time. Why haven't the foxes or the badgers been at him, especially when he was first put underground, because they would get the scent of him right away?"

"Oh, I think I can explain that. You see, I pulled a number of planks away. They were lying in a row, the ends sticking out of the bramble. I took them to shore up the wall after I mended it."

"But it would take some planks to keep a fox out, lad, if he was hungry, especially in the winter."

"There were six of them, big flat ones; they covered quite a space, and I trampled down the undergrowth in getting them out. It was that, I suppose, that cleared the way for Snuffy"— he now shook his head before he ended—"Eeh! but when I look at her, Peter, I just can't believe it."

"Are you frightened of her?"

Davy's expression was slightly shamefaced. "I was for a little while, but then it all went, 'cos . . . 'cos I'm sorry for her. She's . . . she's lonely."

"You sensed that an' all?"

"Aye."

"Aye, she's lonely all right, and it's plain to see you and the nipper there must have been a godsend to her, living in that place alone for years. It's a wonder she didn't go barmy."

"The folk around here think she's a bit odd anyway."

"She's no more odd than you or me, lad. And you know, people stick that word onto you if you don't run to pattern. She's an individualist, an' must always have been."

"A what . . . ?"

"An individualist; you know, somebody who thinks for themselves."

"Oh aye. Yes, I would say she's that all right."

There was silence between them until Davy, looking down at John Willie, who was hanging onto Snuffy, said softly, "She thinks the world of him; she treats him as if he were her own. It makes me feel, well, funny inside sometimes, just to see her with him. Whenever she can she takes his hand."

"God help her."

"What did you say?"

"I said God help her, and the way I see it she'll need His help, because if you're going to stay there with the dog, this business'll come to light sooner or later, that is unless you dig up the body and cart it away someplace and bury it again."

"*Oh no. No.*" Davy almost shrank away. "I couldn't do that, man; it turned me stomach just to look at it."

Again Peter rubbed his hand hard across his chin as he said now, "If I thought it would solve her problem I would go and do it meself, but her problem isn't only a body lying there: it's the fellow who comes and bleeds her. That's her problem."

"Aye, you're right."

"But, seemingly, since she keeps on paying him she wants it to remain her problem. And God only knows what would happen to her if it all came into the open. So, lad, the only solution I see for it is what I said afore, get rid of the body—or the dog. And"—he grinned at Davy—"it goes without saying you won't do that . . . . Now look, don't get alarmed, I'll come along with you. I've never seen a full-sized skeleton afore, although I've seen me share of dead men, but I should guess that one sack will hold what's left of him."

"But what'll you do with him?" Davy's voice was an awed whisper now.

"Take him back in there." Peter jerked his head. "I've had one or two trips inside lately. There are a thousand and one places where he can lie undisturbed until kingdom come, and if he were found, who's to know who he was except that he was a miner . . . a

forgotten miner. . . . What's the best time . . . I mean
when she's out of the road?"

"She's . . . she's never really out of the road"—
Davy's voice had a distinct tremble to it now—"but
she's generally indoors from about eleven o'clock until dinnertime."

"How about early on, right early on?"

"Oh, she's up shortly after me sometimes. It's habit,
I think, an' she's cleanin' the kitchen many a morning
at seven."

"Can you open that hole in the wall again?"

"Aye."

"Can you get it done the morrow?"

"Yes, I'll work it in. She doesn't stand over me to
see what I'm doin', never has done."

"She's unusual in that way an' all then I'd say. Well
now, the following day, Tuesday, I'll . . . I'll come in
around half-past ten. You be there to show me where
the place is, and once I get him gathered together your
worries'll be over. And hers an' all, at least as much
as we can do for her. All right?"

"Aye, all right."

"Don't worry, lad."

"I . . . I can't help it. It seems awful taking him out
of his grave."

"Well, it's either that or Snuffy there presenting her
with part of him. And what would the consequences
of that be, eh? Whatever the mystery is, it lies between
her and Potter. She would likely feel it was the last
straw if she knew you'd got wind of it, and God knows
what it might drive her to. People can only stand so
much, lad. Now go on. Go on, the both of you, and
see Mr. Cartwright, and when you get back try to act
natural like with her. And thank her for the food; aye,
thank her very kindly for that.

"No, no; I don't want that an' all, thanks all the same." Peter was now flapping his hand toward Davy's outstretched one, and Davy, his voice firm, said, "Look, I've more than I know what to do with. I've told you, you can pay me back. An' what's a bob? Go on, man."

Peter slowly took the shilling from Davy's palm and, turning his head to the side, muttered below his breath, "It makes me ashamed to take from a bit of a lad like you."

"Huh!" Davy laughed now as he said airily, "Don't be daft, man. A few weeks ago I'd have pinched the bread out of me grannie's mouth."

Their laughter joined for a moment. Then Davy, motioning to John Willie, said, "So long, Peter."

"So long, lad. See you Tuesday morning if all goes well. In the meantime keep a tight hold on him." He thumbed down toward Snuffy, then patted John Willie's head, and as he did so he looked at Davy and asked quietly, "Do you think he realizes the seriousness of this business?"

"Nobody better."

"Really?"

"Aye, really. He's not daft, you know, Peter."

"I never thought he was, lad."

"I wish I could say that everybody was of the same mind; just because he can neither talk nor hear they dub him as crazy. Sometimes I think he's got more in his noddle than I have."

"I wouldn't say that; no, I wouldn't say that, lad." Peter laughed. "Anyway, be seeing you."

"Aye, be seeing you. . . ."

Davy went to the village and saw Mr. Cartwright and was made very welcome with tea and oven-bottom cake, and Mr. Cartright was very pleased that he and

John Willie had, as he put it, "fallen on their feet." Davy enjoyed his visit, and at the close of the afternoon they left amid kindly farewells and made their way back to the Manor.

Davy had taken a shortcut, not only in order to avoid passing the cottage he had once called home, but in case he might run into any of the Coxons. But he had just emerged from a lane with John Willie and the dog behind him when he met four of them in a bunch.

Mr. Coxon and his three eldest sons were approaching the stile from Farmer Millbanks's field. The three boys were chewing on turnips, and Mr. Coxon was lashing out with a long switch at dead fronds of bracken that were growing by the side of the ditch. On sighting the little party ahead of him, his hand became still and he stared fixedly at Davy, as did his sons.

Davy, standing his ground, stared back. Under ordinary circumstances he would have stood no chance against the three Coxon boys, who would have been egged into a fight by their father; but now, his head up, he looked this man boldly in the eye, and Mr. Coxon received the message written plainly in Davy's disdainful glance, and with a growl of, "Come on, get over there," he thrust his boys one after the other over the stile. But as he himself mounted it he began lashing out wildly with the switch; yet he was wise enough to keep it just clear of Davy's face.

Although he had put on a bold front, Davy heaved a sigh of relief when they were on the other side of the stile. Yet in the short space of time when he and Matthew Coxon confronted each other, he knew that the battle had been won. But it had really been won the other night around the table in the Manor kitchen, hadn't it?

Again he heaved a sigh. That was another obstacle over. Lor! but he hated that fellow, and all of his tribe. . . . That was another thing. She, Miss Peamarsh, she hated him an' all. She hadn't only been fighting his battle the other night; she had been fighting one of her own. Now why? Why? His mind gave him no clue to this question.

But now, he told himself, he must think what he was going to say to her, what excuse he was going to give for locking Snuffy in the woodshed all day the morrow. And what would he say to her tonight? How could he act natural with her, knowing what he knew about her?

A quarter of an hour later, after letting himself through the gate—she had entrusted him with another key—he went up the drive, across the yard, and put Snuffy in the woodshed. Then wiping his feet well and bidding John Willie do the same, he tapped on the door and entered the kitchen.

In the lamplight he saw her sitting before the fire, and he thought that her mind must have taken her miles away, because she did not immediately turn round toward them as she usually did. When she did become aware of them she rose quickly to her feet and smiled as she said, "Well, there you are, back then. Have you had a nice day?" And without waiting for Davy to answer she bent down to John Willie and repeated, "Have you had a nice day?" motioning with her hands in a waving movement, and he nodded and smiled at her and answered, "Huh."

"Good. Good. I suppose you are hungry?" Now she was addressing Davy, and he found it easy to say lightly, "I'm always hungry, miss."

"Did you see your friends?"

"Aye. Yes, I saw Mr. and Mrs. Cartwright, and Peter . . . Mr. Talbot."

"How are they? Mr. Talbot, is he still living in the mine?"

"Yes, miss, an' . . . an' he's all right."

"Well now, the tea's all ready." She pointed to the table, and he saw it was all ready, quite a big spread. "Have you washed your hands?"

"No; I'm sorry, miss."

"Well, do them at the sink; be quick now."

Davy took John Willie with him to the sink, and while they washed their hands she said, "Does Mr. Talbot intend to live in the mine all the winter?"

"If he stays, miss, yes; that's all there is for him."

"You said there was no hope of his being given employment around here?"

"Well, there isn't, miss, or in any of the pits near. As he said, he's on the blacklist, and that spreads a long way in the pits. He was telling me he was thinkin' of going down to the south country and trying farmin'."

"Farming?" She had turned from the fire with the kettle in her hand and looked at him where he was standing at the far side of the table waiting to be told that he could sit, and she said, "It's a big step from mining to farming."

"Well, as I understand, miss, he was a farmer originally; at least his father was; they had a farm of their own."

"Indeed!" She mashed the tea from the boiling kettle.

"Yes, miss, he was gone sixteen when he first went down the pit. His father went broke and they had to sell everything. He was ailing, his father, with the consumption, and his mother went an' all the next year."

She stood looking at him, still holding the heavy kettle in her hand. And then after a pause she said, "How sad for him. He has no people?"

"No, he's a loner. That's what he calls himself, a loner."

"Yes, yes." She had her back to him again as she said, "Yes, yes, I can understand that, a loner. Well now, be seated"—she came briskly to the table—"and tell me all the gossip you have heard today."

So he found himself telling her the little bits of news he had heard in the Cartwrights' kitchen; then he told her about the meeting with Mr. Coxon and his sons, and this brought from her a deep "Ah! Ah!"

The tea over, the table cleared, the dishes washed, she said to him suddenly, "We are going to have a reading tonight. I am going to read to you from the Bible."

He watched her leave the room, then kept his puzzled gaze on the door until she returned. She was going to read from the Bible, but she had scoffed at what the minister had said about God!

Laying a big leather-bound brass-clasped book on the table, she looked at him as if she were apologizing to him for something as she said, "It . . . it is a long time since I read from the Bible, but your encounter with Mr. Coxon demands I read you a representative story. I suppose it should really be about David slaying the Philistine Goliath, but no, I feel that one of the Psalms would be appropriate, and if I remember rightly perhaps the fifty-sixth."

Davy watched her thumbing through the thin pages of the great book. So far he couldn't follow anything she had said; it was as if she were talking in a foreign language.

And then, after looking at him she said, "This Psalm is about David praying to God and God telling him that He has confidence in him." Then, her head slightly to the side, her eyes cast down, she began:

Be merciful unto me, O God:
for man would swallow me up;
he fighting daily oppresseth me.

Mine enemies would daily swallow me up:
for they be many that fight against me,
O thou most High.

What time I am afraid,
I will trust in thee.

On and on she went. He could not understand the sense of it all, but he liked the sound of her voice. It was as if she were saying a song rather than singing it.

When I cry unto thee,
then shall my enemies turn back:
this I know; for God is for me.

There was more and more, until she ended:

For thou hast delivered my soul from death:
wilt not thou deliver my feet from falling,
that I may walk before God in the light of the living?

They were staring at each other. The wick of the lamp spluttered slightly and he blinked as he repeated to himself, "That I may walk before God in the light of the living."

She hadn't let her brother walk before God, had she? But her face in the lamplight was soft and kind. She looked happy, as happy as he'd ever seen her.

John Willie was gazing at her, his eyes wide, and she looked at him in silence for a moment before impulsively thrusting out her hand and clasping his where they lay joined on top of the table almost underneath his chin. And when he saw them exchange a glance which radiated a strange warmth, he again experienced that weak sensation in his throat and became petrified that in the next minute he'd give way to this rising weakness.

When he sprang up from the table and went toward the sink, she said, "What is it?" and he answered thickly, "I . . . I'd just like a drink of water, miss."

There was a moment's silence before she spoke again. And then she said softly, "Yes, yes, I understand, David. I too have been affected in my time. There is great beauty in the Bible."

Eeh! she didn't understand anything, not a thing. She was getting everything wrong. But let her think she understood, let her if it made her happy.

As he pumped the water into the mug he thought that perhaps, after all, it wasn't such a good thing that she had taken them in and fed and sheltered them, because this very fact might become her undoing; and he had the idea that if she were now to be parted from John Willie she would in some way lose the spring of life. Now where had he heard that saying? Aw, he didn't know, but it fitted the case, anyway.

Nine

"That's it." Davy pointed to the roughly turned earth. "I put the planks back on it last night because the top had been disturbed an' it wasn't Snuffy this time."

Peter stood for a moment looking down on the strange grave before he said, "Well, lad, let's get going. By the way, where's the young 'un?"

"He's with the miss in . . . in the kitchen; she thinks he's got a cold comin'. She's always watchful of him an' his colds since the do he had in the summer-house." He nodded toward the little building.

"Just as well. We'll work quicker on our own. So, here goes."

A few minutes later Peter straightened his back and drew his teeth tightly over his bottom lip as he stared down on the gaping skull. Then he spoke to it, saying, "You poor devil. I don't suppose we'll ever know the reason why you're lying there." He turned to Davy now. "I think we'd better clear all the soil off first, eh? Then pack the long bones in the sack, an' leave his skull till last. Out of a sort of overdue respect, let's say, for if it was me I'd still want me head on top."

And so, kneeling one each side of the grave, they began to rake the earth away from the bones with their hands. Some pieces of earth had formed into clots, and they lifted these out whole and put them to one side.

It was as they were uncovering the leg bones below the thighs that they both became frozen into stillness. Their backs bent, their hands in the shallow grave, neither of them lifted his head, yet their eyes slanted toward each other as they became aware of the presence near them. It was a cry as if from a strangled throat that almost brought them tumbling into each other's arms and onto the skeleton. Then again they became frozen as they looked up at Miss Peamarsh standing with her back to the corner of the summer-house, her two hands gripping her throat, her mouth wide agape, while her head fell farther and farther back onto her shoulders as if she were actually being strangled.

Peter uttered no word as he sprang up and forward and caught the tottering figure as it fell toward the ground.

"Oh my God! my God!"

Still without a word, Peter laid her down on the rough earth, and now Davy was kneeling by her side gripping her hands as he gabbled, "Is she dead? Eeh! what have I done? If she dies it'll be my fault. She was in the kitchen, she was. She hadn't twigged anything. I acted normal, like you said . . ."

"Be quiet, lad! Be quiet!" Peter's ear was now resting on Miss Peamarsh's breast, and then he said, "I think she's just fainted, but . . . but I can hardly hear anything. Look, help me; help hoist her up and I'll carry her to the house."

Within minutes they were stumbling through the overgrown orchard, Peter with Miss Peamarsh in his arms, while Davy supported her head. When they rested for a moment against the back of a garden seat, Miss Peamarsh gave a shuddering breath, lifted her head, opened her eyes and looked into Peter's face; then once more she fainted away.

When at last they entered the kitchen and Peter had laid her on the settle, he turned to Davy, saying, "Does she keep any spirits or anything in the house?"

"No, not that I know of. A cordial . . . she calls it a cordial, in the cupboard there."

"Get it."

When Davy brought the bottle, Peter took out the cork, smelled it, put his tongue to it and, with a grimace, said, "That's no good, cough mixture." Then taking up a news sheet, he handed it to Davy, saying, "Roll that up tight and light it at the fire."

"Light the paper?"

"Aye, do as I say, lad; light the paper. Then stamp it out and give it to me quick."

Mystified, Davy did as he was bidden; then he watched Peter waft the black smoking paper under Miss Peamarsh's nose. Some seconds later when she began to cough, he himself coughed, not only from the smoke which had got into his throat, but also with relief.

He stood now and looked down on Miss Peamarsh as she slowly opened her eyes, and she stared back at him, holding his gaze deeply and in sorrow. Then her eyes moved from his and up to the man standing at her feet, and her gaze fell from his as he said, "I'm

. . . I'm sorry. We . . . we were only doing what we thought was for the best. The . . . the animal had found it . . . you understand?"

She made no movement whatever, and Peter, still looking down on her, murmured, "You have no need to worry about me or the lad. He's . . . he's known for some time, and . . . and he wanted to do what was best for you. That's all."

Again she was looking at Davy, and, her head making small, almost imperceivable movements, she whispered, "Oh, David, David." Then she closed her eyes tightly, and when he saw the tears pressing themselves from beneath her lids, there once more came into his throat that feeling of weakness, and he turned his face away, and Peter said, "Make a cup of tea, strong."

Almost gratefully, Davy busied himself with the tea-making, and when it was ready Miss Peamarsh was sitting up on the settle.

As Davy placed the cup of tea into her hands he could not help but notice that she seemed changed, perhaps because she wasn't, as usual, sitting bolt upright. Her body was slumped, all of it, even her face; it was as if the props that had supported her had been whipped away.

Slowly she sipped at the tea, and no one spoke until she had finished drinking. Then, handing the cup to Davy, she said quietly, "Thank you," after which she turned her gaze upon Peter, and, her voice still quiet, seemingly without life, she said, "Would you please sit down, and you too, David?" Then just as Davy sat down she made a motion with her hand, saying, "I'm sorry; would you mind calling John Willie? He is gathering the eggs. I . . . I would like him to hear what I've got to say. Yes"—she nodded at Davy now, and her voice slow and tired-sounding she said, "I know you will remind me that he can't hear, but I also know the child is aware of everything I say, and I want him particularly to understand, for he has been troubled these last few days. I have known there was something on his mind, as on yours. Go now and bring him, please."

Quickly Davy went from the kitchen; then at a gallop he raced across the yard and to the field where the hens were, and he pulled John Willie from the hen run, crying, "Come on! Come on!"

"Huh. Huh."

"Never mind why; come on." Without further explanation Davy ran him back to the house and into the kitchen, and there, both of them panting, he made him sit on the stool facing Miss Peamarsh.

It had been evident to Davy as he entered the kitchen that Peter had been talking to Miss Peamarsh, but now they all sat looking at her in silence where she sat staring at her joined hands while her fingers plucked at each other. It was a full minute before she spoke and then slowly she began:

"I will start at the beginning. When I was young, a child, this house was a happy house. I . . . my brother and I were brought up and educated here. I was two years older than my brother. My mother loved her only son very dearly; I loved him too, and my father loved him, but . . . but my brother cared only for my mother and himself. Yet we were all very happy together until my mother died. I was thirteen years old at the time, and when she went I took her place in the household. My brother"—she paused here and swallowed deeply before going on—"he . . . he missed my mother very much, and my father thought it wise to send him away to school. He would have done so much earlier, only my mother became distressed every time the subject was mentioned."

Now she drew out a long sigh and, raising her head a little, looked at Davy. "When my brother—his name was Richard—ran away from school for the third time, my father gave up trying to force him and he tried to tutor him himself. My father, by the way, was an elderly man." She glanced toward Peter now. "He had married late in life. But all his life he had worked very hard and he was loved and respected by everyone who knew him. He never refused a helping hand to anyone in his life. As . . . as my brother grew older, my father became much more worried about him because he would not settle to any career and . . . and he was given to drinking. He had been drinking secretly since he had returned home at the age of sixteen." She now directed her gaze toward Davy again. "Our friend Mr. Coxon had, I understand, an illicit still somewhere in the hills. It was he who introduced my brother to this cheap raw liquor and used to keep him supplied with it."

She now took a handkerchief from her skirt pocket and wiped her mouth with it, and as she did so Peter Talbot said softly, "You've got no need to go on, miss."

"Thank you, Mr. Talbot, but I would rather."

When he made a slight movement of assent with his head, she continued, "My father's stipend as a parson was very small but he had a private income. At the time I am speaking of it was almost swallowed up with paying my brother's debts. Then one night"—she now straightened her back and pressed her shoulders against the settle as she repeated—"one night a man came from Gateshead. It . . . it was a very raw night

in late December. I can see him now. There was snow
on the back of his hair and on his moustache. He was
the father of a little maid we . . . we had had. She was
a sweet child and she had left our service some seven
months earlier. Her father had come to tell us that she
had died in childbed and the baby with her, and only
with her last breath had she named the father of the
child."

Her back still pressed against the settle, she went
on, "My father was a gentle man, gentle in every sense
of the word. I had never known him to lose his temper,
but that night when my brother came in the worse for
drink, there . . . there was a dreadful scene. When my
father told him of the man's visit and that he must
make reparation for the sin he had committed, my
brother laughed at him; he sneered at him and made
ridicule of his religion and all the work that he had
done in his life. It was too much. I saw something burst
in my father, and he sprang on his only son and struck
him, not with his hand only but with a bronze figure,
a statuette which he had whipped up from a table that
was near to his hand. The blow felled my brother, but
it might not have killed him had he not fallen into the
fireplace and crushed his temple against the pro-
truding firedog."

The kitchen had become very quiet. There was no
sound, not even that of breathing, until she sighed and
said, "It was my screams that brought Potter in. He
hadn't far to come; he must have been listening outside the door; it was a habit of his. It was as we lifted
my brother from the fireplace that my father collapsed. He had a stroke, and he never spoke from that
moment until the day he died, which was two years
later.

"I . . . I was overwhelmed. My brother was dead,

quite dead, and although my father was desperately ill I thought he would recover and that when he did, the consequences he was likely to suffer for his act were something I couldn't bear to think about. It . . . it was Potter who put forward an idea. Mr. Richard, he said, had been saying for a long time he was going abroad; in fact he had told people in the inn only the night before of his plan to travel. So why not let it be thought he had gone abroad; it would save the master disgrace. He would hint, as it were, that Master Richard had told him he was going to foreign parts, and so"—she spread her hands in front of her now—"I . . . I did as he suggested. And I must say now that at the time I was only too pleased to fall in with his plan, for it was unthinkable that my father, that good man who had worked for others all his life, should at his age have to face a public court and the consequences of his deed. But . . . but in my anxiety and gratitude to Potter I made a mistake; I doubled his wages and those of his wife. Perhaps the idea of blackmail was already in his mind, but my action precipitated it. It was the day after my father's funeral that he came into the open and told me the price I had to pay for his silence, and I have been paying it on the first Monday of each quarter ever since."

"The damned scoundrel! Excuse me, miss." Peter Talbot had risen to his feet. "If he was here this minute there'd be another hole needed to be dug, I can tell you that. And I'll tell you something else, miss, and I must say it. I think you've been very foolish; you should have let the matter come into the open, at least after your father died. People would have understood."

"No, Mr. Talbot, people wouldn't have understood. They would have said, What! Parson Peamarsh, a man of God who had preached forgiveness all his life, whose favorite sermon was the prodigal son, had killed his own son because he took a glass too much and because he had . . . Well"—she cast a quick glance in Davy's direction—"he had sinned against another! Where was the forgiving father? they would have said. Most ignorant people, and many who classed themselves as their betters, would have called him a hypocrite, a mealymouthed hypocrite. And because of this their very faith would have been tested and found wanting. Also they would have remembered that my brother had been a very likable individual. And that was true, for he was not a bad man; weak and self-indulgent, but not really bad." She sighed deeply here. The stiffness seeped from her back and she slumped in the seat again before she said, "When I blame myself for my own weakness, I look back to that time, and I can see that I couldn't have taken any other course than that on which I decided."

"But it's all over now, miss."

To Peter's remark she now made a sound similar to that of John Willie's huh, then said, "Nothing's changed, as I see it, only that two more people . . . no, three"—she glanced softly down on John Willie—"know the reason for my isolation."

"You can't go on like this, miss."

She turned her head now and looked at Peter. "You think not, Mr. Talbot?"

"I do, miss. This has got to be brought into the open."

"That would seem to you to be a very easy solution, but what you are not taking into account, Mr. Talbot, is that it is only my word now against Potter's. There are no other witnesses to prove, as he once pointed out, that it wasn't myself who took up the bronze ornament and attacked my brother with it. He even went fully into how he would represent his version, saying that on my father's cry he had come into the room and found me bending over my brother with the implement in my hand while my father was near collapse. I, in turn, told him that when that state of affairs was reached he would undoubtedly be in prison for blackmail, and his answer to this was, 'But, miss, just think; it wouldn't do you much good, would it, knowing I was in prison, because you'd be in the same boat?' "She looked wearily at Peter now as she asked, "How do you propose that I prove my innocence?"

"When is he coming again, miss?"

"What did you say, David?"

"I said when is he coming again, miss?"

"He usually comes, as I said, on the first Monday of the quarter, but he made an unexpected visit a short while ago and demanded a hundred pounds for some scheme he has in mind. When I told him I hadn't the money he proposed that I sell some of the china or cameos from the drawing room. He said he would give me two weeks to think about it. Today is"—she paused —"Tuesday; he will be here on Friday."

When she had finished speaking, silence again fell upon them, and during it John Willie, leaving Davy's side, went to her and, hitching himself onto the settle, sat close beside her. And when he took her hand she looked down on him tenderly, saying, "Dear John Willie." Then casting her glance over Davy and Peter, she said, "I told you he understands. Yes indeed; he understands many things, does John Willie." As she turned and looked down on the boy again Davy said abruptly, "The parson. The parson, miss; you've got to tell the parson, and . . . and he'll bring a Justice and . . . and they could hide in the drawin' room like I . . . ."

There was a long pause before Miss Peamarsh said, "Hide in the drawing room like you did? When, David?"

He had his head bowed as he replied, "The day he came, Potter. I heard you call out an' I thought he was up to something, an' I went into the hall and stood in the drawing-room doorway, and I heard bits and pieces. Then . . . then when you came out, quick like I slipped into the drawing room."

Miss Peamarsh and Peter now exchanged quick glances; then, looking at Davy again, she said, "And knowing all this, and what it surely implied, you stayed on?" Her eyes lifting to Peter, she said, "There are things that happen in life, Mr. Talbot, that renew one's faith in God and His plan for all of us."

"Aye, I suppose you could say that, miss, if you were of that turn of mind."

"You're not?"

"No, not really, miss. God as I can see Him has done little for man except to set him at his brother's throat, and He's cast His favors where the favors were already bountiful. It's all the way one looks at it, miss."

"Yes, yes, it's all the way one looks at it. And how do you look at David's proposed scheme?"

"I think it's very sensible, miss, and that it's what you should do, and without further delay."

"But have you thought that if the Justice was seen coming in here, Potter would have wind of it before he passed through the village? There's nothing goes unnoticed in the village."

"Oh, there's ways and means, miss, of getting him in. We could work that out. The hole in the wall, for instance, could be made big enough to take a walking man."

"Then what?"

"Well, as the lad here said, miss, put them in your drawing room and leave the door slightly ajar, and also the one in the room from which you're speaking, and once you're in the room they could leave the drawing room and do what Davy did, stand outside the door and listen. It would be up to you to lead the talk round so that he would convict himself."

"It sounds all too simple."

"And it could be if you set to work straightaway, miss. Davy could go for the parson now and I'll see to making a doorway through the wall an', an' rectifying other things." He moved his head slowly.

"It's very kind of you, Mr. Talbot."

"Will I go now, miss?" Davy was standing in front of her, his face eager, his body taut as if ready to run.

She looked at him, deep into his face, before she said softly, "Yes, David, go and get the parson." Then she lay back and closed her eyes while she put her arm around John Willie's shoulder and drew him tightly against her as she murmured, "I feel I'm being born again. It's a strange sensation, a very strange sensation."

Ten

Parson Murray could hardly believe his ears. And the Justice too after he had been led, not without protest, through the rough bramble path and the hole in the wall could hardly believe his ears, but both of them said the same thing to Miss Peamarsh in Davy's hearing: "You have been a very foolish woman." And the parson had added, "You would have gone down to your own grave impoverished and lonely if God had not guided those two boys to you. Aye, the ways of God are indeed strange, indeed; indeed, they are."

For the next two days the house was all abustle with comings and goings. Parson Murray paid four secret visits, and the Justice, again led through the wall by Peter, returned the second day with a clerk who wrote out a long statement from Miss Peamarsh, and with this the stage was all set for the morning of Friday, October 31.

Davy rose at five o'clock. The air was bitterly cold and he scrambled into his clothes in the dark. He did not waken John Willie; he always gave him another hour after he himself rose, when generally he roused him with a hot drink.

As he groped his way past the window toward the door he stopped. There, across the yard, he could see a light on in the kitchen, which meant that the miss was up.

He crept slowly down the dark well of the staircase and into the yard, and he shivered as the frosty cold air struck him. He didn't usually go to the house until seven o'clock, by which time he had mucked out the cowshed, drawn the water, lit his own fire and done several other odd jobs. But this morning he made his way straight to the kitchen door and knocked on it gently.

"Come in, David."

It was almost as if she had been expecting him. She was sitting in the corner of the settle close to the fire, which was glowing brightly as if it had been bellowed some time ago.

"You're . . . you're up early, miss?"

"I couldn't sleep. I have just made fresh tea; help yourself."

"Thank you, miss."

When he stood by the table, the mug in his hand, she said to him, "Sit down, David," and he sat down and stared at her. She looked as different again this morning from how she had done yesterday, and from all the days that had gone before, and her voice too was different; the sharp edge had gone entirely from it. "Do you know, David, this may be the most important day in my life."

"Yes, miss."

"And . . . and if things turn out as well as all is planned I will be a free woman once again. Can you understand that, David? I will be a free woman."

Yes, he could understand that, but he didn't answer her; he merely nodded, until she said, "And it's all thanks to you." Then he was quick to reply, "Oh no, miss. It . . . it was bound to come out in the open sooner or later. Give a man like Potter enough rope and he'll hang himself."

"I'm sorry to have to contradict you, David, but men like Potter don't usually hang themselves; they're too wily. It is others who must put the rope around their necks, and you have done this; at least if I am able to act the part this morning, you will have accomplished it."

"You'll act your part, miss, never fear."

She now turned her head away from him and looked into the fire, and after a while she said, "Will you continue to work for me, David?"

"Oh aye. Yes, miss."

"I mean when the summer comes or when there is a prospect of work in the pit again, will you still consider working for me?"

He paused a minute while he thought. Even if everything went as she said, according to plan, she'd still be lonely. John Willie had filled the gap a bit, but if he was to take him away. . . . "Yes, miss, I'll work for you as long as you want."

She was looking at him again. "Even if I was not able to pay you a full wage?"

Unhesitatingly he now said, "Aye, miss: I'm content with what I've got."

"You're easily satisfied, David."

"Oh no, I'm not, miss, I've got ideas an' wants. But . . . but I owe you a big debt, an' I'll stay as long as you need me."

They stared at each other while the wall clock ticked the seconds away, and the fire spluttered, and the lamp began to smoke just the slightest. Then she turned her face from him as she said, "I've had a plan in mind for some time. It . . . it was merely a piece of wishful thinking at first, but now, well, after today maybe it could become reality. It will all depend on you, David." She turned her head toward him again, saying, "We will discuss it later."

She rose to her feet, her voice brisk now but not sharp. "We're almost out of bread. I got nothing done yesterday; I must bake, and . . . and there'll likely be company for tea." She smiled at him, and he smiled back and said, "I hope so, miss." Then as he went toward the door she asked a question that brought him round abruptly to face her. "Do you like Mr. Talbot, David?"

"Oh aye, miss, I think he's a grand blo . . . fellow . . . man, I mean."

"He's a man you could trust, you would say?"

"Oh aye, miss, yes. And he's got principles, I'd say, high ones, else he wouldn't be out of work at this minute and blacklisted."

She nodded toward him now and said, "Yes, one must suffer for one's principles. When he comes later, as arranged, you must take him into your rooms and give him something to eat and drink. He will need it; it's a bitter morning."

"Thank you, miss; he'll be grateful."

As he went toward the door she turned toward the fireplace, and he caught her words, but he didn't quite follow them. "It's difficult for the poor who are proud and arrogant to be grateful." He couldn't really see where that description fitted Peter, yet he felt she was alluding to him.

At ten o'clock that morning Peter Talbot once again led Justice MacIntyre and the parson through the narrow path between the bramble and the Manor wall, then through the hole which he had made into an opening five feet high, leaving the top coping stones in place. When they came to the grave beside the summerhouse they stood in silence for a moment looking down on it. Then they went on through the rough orchard toward the house.

When they reached the yard the parson, turning to Peter, said, "I'd be obliged if you would remain near at hand, for neither myself nor the Justice here would be much good in a bout of fisticuffs. And as I remember Dan Potter he was a sturdily built man, and a cornered man can become like a cornered animal, vicious."

"Well, I hope he'll put up a fight, sir, for it would give me the greatest pleasure in the world to get me hands on the fellow."

The Justice now smiled at Peter, saying, "Well, if you get your wish, leave enough of him for the law to deal with, won't you?" Then he and the parson went toward the front door, where Miss Peamarsh was awaiting them like, Davy thought, the lady of the house should do, except that she didn't look like the lady of the house, for within the last hour she had changed her clothes and was now dressed in the old stained skirt and washed-out blouse that he had first seen her in.

Davy scampered across the yard now and hailed

Peter, saying, "There's grub . . . a meal ready for you, she left it all set. Just a minute, I'll fetch it and we'll go over to my place." It was odd, but it was the first time he had called the rooms his place. It had a nice sound, as if he were settled for life.

A few minutes later he came hurrying from the kitchen with a tray on which there were two plates of food, one covered with a tureen lid, the other piled high with new bread, and beside them stood a steaming pot of tea.

"That for me?" Peter looked down at the tray.

"Aye. She said you were to have it. She's got it ready."

Davy watched Peter nip on his lower lip, then jerk his head to the side as if in slight bewilderment; then on a laugh he said, "Well, what are we waiting for?" and now, their laughter joined, they went toward the stable.

"Where's the nipper?" Peter asked as they mounted the stairs.

"He's in bed. He had a bit of a cough and I just happened to mention it to her and she was over here like lightnin', an' she made him take his clothes off again and get into bed. I'm tellin' you'—he pulled a face at Peter now—"he's being spoiled. There'll be no holding him shortly; he'll expect to be waited on like the gentry."

"And why not? . . . Aw, this is nice, comfortable." Peter stood looking round the room. "You've fallen on your feet here, lad. Not that you don't deserve it."

"Aye, I'm lucky, an' I know it. She asked me this morning if I'd like to stay on, I mean for good."

"And you said?"

"Aye."

"That's right, you and the nipper'll be a comfort to

her, company. An' that's what she needs. A woman like her should have been married years ago, with a family of her own, but I doubt if she'll take that step now, so I'm glad she's got you both. Me mind'll drift back to you time and again in the future. . . ."

"What do you mean, your mind'll drift back?"

"Well, I told you I was for going down south, didn't I? I would have been away afore now if this business hadn't cropped up. Sunday, when you came over, I'd made up me mind then, so I'm going the morrow."

"The morrow?" Davy shook his head. "Aw, I'll miss you, man. I've . . . I've never had a real pal. An' me da. . . . Well, me da hadn't much patience with young 'uns."

"And I'll miss you, lad. . . . Funny how we met up, isn't it, breaking stones in the workhouse?"

They looked at each other in awkward silence until Peter laughingly said, "And now we end up catching a blackmailer. Aw, I'm looking forward to gettin' me hands on that bloke. To think what he's got off with all these years, sucking her dry like that, turning her into an old woman afore her time . . . . She must have been bonny years ago."

"Aye, I thought that meself. The other day when she let go like and forgot to be stiff, she looked young like."

"Well"—Peter now raised his mug of hot tea and said—"here's to the end of Potter and a new beginnin' for her. What do you say, lad?"

"I say with you, Peter, a new beginning for her."

"Good. And now we only have to wait for the gate bell to ring."

Eleven

It was exactly eleven o'clock when the bell rang, and as if it were a signal for battle they all went to their posts: the parson and the Justice into the drawing room, and Miss Peamarsh to the kitchen, where she set about preparing vegetables for the dinner as she would have done on an ordinary day; Peter went and stood within the door of the cow-byre where he could see and not be seen, and Davy walked down the drive to open the gate. He did not run, he did not hurry, he just walked, and when he reached the gate and inserted the key in the lock Dan Potter looked at him through the bars and said, "You didn't take a word of warnin', did you, lad?"

"What d'you mean?" It was Davy's part in the affair to appear none too bright, even slightly stupid, and Dan Potter treated him as such when he said, "Are you daft? Remember me last words to you? I told you to

166

get yourself goin'. An' I'll tell you again, 'tisn't healthy for you here. Do you know that?''

"No."

They were walking up the drive, a good arm's length between them, but Dan Potter lessened the space as they drew near the yard, and now, his tone changing, he said, "I'm speakin' for your own good, lad. Unless you want trouble I'd get onto the road again. You don't know what you're riskin' stayin' here, alone with her.''

"No?"

"No. She's got a mad temper."

"Eeh! has she? I hadn't noticed."

"Then you're dafter than you look."

Davy lowered his head and clenched his teeth for a moment. He hated that word; it was often applied to John Willie and it made him fighting mad. He had to caution himself now to go steady.

Then his whole mind was lifted from Dan Potter and onto John Willie, whom he now saw standing in the doorway of the cow-byre, exclaiming loudly in huhs. He must have got tired of being alone and got into his things, and in passing the cow-byre he had caught sight of Peter.

"Who's he yapping to?" Potter's whole body was stiffly alert.

"Yapping? Nobody. There's . . . there's nobody there."

"Then who's he yapping to?"

"Likely the cow."

Dan Potter stared toward the cow-byre, seemingly not convinced by Davy's explanation, and the next moment he would have crossed the yard if the kitchen door hadn't opened.

Miss Peamarsh, wiping her hands on a towel, looked

at Potter coldly, and he turned his attention from John Willie, and now, with an oily smile, he approached her, saying, "Aw, there you are, miss. And how are you the day?"

"I am as well as can be expected." She turned her back on him, walked across the kitchen, folded up the towel and hung it on the brass rod hanging below the mantelpiece; then without further words she went out into the hall, and he followed her.

Davy waited until the kitchen door had closed behind them, then stealthily he tiptoed across the kitchen and paused a moment listening until the sound of Dan Potter's voice had almost faded away, by which time he knew they had entered the study.

Quickly now he took off his clogs, and in his stockinged feet he entered the hall and soundlessly made his way to the drawing-room door, which he cautiously opened without making a sound, for last night he had oiled the hinges well. Silently he beckoned to the parson and the Justice, where they were standing opposite the empty fireplace, looking somewhat odd and shorter in stature, for they too had taken the precaution of removing their boots.

Cautiously too they came toward him, and as cautiously they took up their positions, one at each side of the study door, while Davy stood between them in front of it. The first words they heard clearly were, "I gave you a fortnight to think better on it."

"And I have thought better on it, as you say, and I'm not going to meet your new demand. And what is more, I will tell you at this moment I am regretting that I ever took your advice. If I had sent for the Justice of the Peace in the first place they would have dealt leniently with my father, for as you well know he had no intention of killing his son; he struck a blow at him, but it was the firedog that caused the fatality."

"You're being silly, miss—excuse me saying so—for Justices being what they are, they would have reasoned that Master Richard would never have reached the firedog if Parson hadn't struck him with the bronze statuette. They may not have hanged him, but he would surely have gone along the line. You know that as well as me. An' what's more, you were the one who was anxious to keep your father's good name unblemished, now weren't you, miss? Quite hysterical you were about it as I recall. 'Anything,' you said; 'I'll do anything, Potter, to save me father from the consequences of tonight.' That's what you said to me, miss, in the room next door. 'Help me, Potter,' you said; 'help me.' "

"And you did help me, didn't you? You have helped me all these years by blackmailing me, by turning this house into a haunted place. Well, it is finished, Potter, quite finished."

"Now! now! miss. Don't get hasty. Remember what I told you once before. It won't do much good you bringin' the facts to light at this stage, 'cos I warned you of what I'd do if driven to it, didn't I? And I will, I'll swear on the good Book that I saw your hand strike that blow. An' they'll believe me, for nobody, they'd reason, would be mad enough to pay just to keep a dead man's name clear. Although I might have to suffer, I won't be sufferin' alone; I'll have that consolation. An' this house that you're so fond of will indeed become haunted, for it'll drop into rack and ruin. . . ."

. . ."I don't think so, Daniel Potter. I don't think so."

The door had been thrown back so forcibly that it crashed against a chair, and in the doorway stood framed the Justice and the parson, with Davy behind them. They all watched the blood drain from Dan Potter's face before he turned his startled gaze from them and glowered on Miss Peamarsh.

"Trap! You've led me into a trap, but you won't get away with it. I swear . . ."

"You'll swear to nothing except to admit that you are a blackmailer and a scoundrel. Daniel Potter, I arrest you in the name of the law."

Potter's mouth was wide open, his jaw hanging loose; his eyes darted from one to the other as if he still couldn't believe what had happened to him. He half swung round looking for a way of escape, and there behind him was a long window leading onto the side terrace. His head jerking back again and his hand going inside his coat, he cried, "Don't move, any of you; don't move!" Like lightning he brought from his pocket a short pistol and, his arm outstretched now, pointed it toward them.

Backing toward the window, he stooped sideward and pulled it up; then, his eyes again flashing from one to the other, he growled, "Me aim is good, so don't attempt to follow me. It isn't the first time I've used this." Then as he was about to step over the low sill he stopped. "The key . . . the gate key. Hand it over, lad. Throw it here, an' quick!"

"I'll . . . I'll not . . . No!"

He was standing inside the room again, the gun directed toward Davy's head. "I'll count three."

"Give him the key, David."

When Davy made no response to Miss Peamarsh's demand, she cried at him with a note of panic in her voice now, while not taking her eyes from Potter, "Give him the key, I say!"

Davy threw the key, but not with any force, and it

landed about a yard from Potter's feet. Quickly thrusting out his leg, he drew the key toward him and, stooping, grabbed it up. And once again he backed out of the window, only now to let out a strangled cry as his free arm was twisted behind him. Before he knew what was happening to him he was thrown onto the dirt of the drive. But he still had hold of the gun, and as Peter bent down to grab him once more, he fired.

The bullet ripping through the top of Peter's coat staggered him, and, gripping his shoulder, he backed away. Potter was now kneeling with the gun leveled at Peter, and froth spurted from his mouth as he growled, "I won't miss next time."

It was as Potter pulled himself to his feet and faced them all, where they stood like a tableau staring at him, that John Willie came running around the corner and straight into his path. Potter didn't seem to glance at the boy before his hand went out and grabbed the collar of his coat, and the action caused John Willie to wriggle and let out a scream of loud and fear-filled huhs.

"Leave him alone. D'you hear? Leave him alone!"

Miss Peamarsh grabbed hold of Davy's arms and held tightly onto him, preventing him from rushing at Potter, while Potter cried, "I'll leave him alone as long as you all stay where you are. If any of you move . . . well, in for a penny, in for a pound." With this he began to back away from them toward the drive, pulling John Willie with him as he went.

At this point the Justice seemed to come out of his stupor and he called, "You won't get far, my man; the constabulary will find you. We will have you."

Potter's reply was lost on them as he hoisted John Willie, who was kicking and punching ineffectively at him, up under his arm.

"Stay still!" Peter thrust out his hand and checked Davy. "Don't worry, we'll head him off. He won't get far. . . . Look, once he gets around the bend of the drive I'll follow him. He won't take his cart through the village, not with the child struggling like that, so he'll make for the fell road. You skip through the wall and wait at the corner. I should be close behind the cart when it reaches there. I'll go up the ditch side, behind the scrub. But if I don't reach the corner in time, don't do anything on your own, for he's a dangerous man. He's likely to shoot you down. As he said, in for a penny, in for a pound. Ah! he's gone. Away with you."

As they both sprang forward Miss Peamarsh's voice followed them, calling, "Be careful. Oh, be careful." Then her voice came to Davy faintly, almost in entreaty, "David. David. Oh, be careful, David."

As he tore through the orchard, past the summer-house and the grave, to the wall, his mind did not seem to be racing with him; in some strange way it appeared to be outside himself, and he listened to it as if someone else were talking to him and saying, "If he does him any harm I'll kill him. If he harms our John Willie, then I'll kill him. John Willie is special. She know's he's special; she's always known he's special. There's goodness in John Willie; locked inside him there's goodness."

He was through the wall and the scrub path, and there in the distance was the road, but as he raced over the fell toward it Potter's cart thundered past the corner. He saw him perched on the edge of the high raised seat at the front. But there was no sign of John Willie, unless he was holding him down with his feet.

When he reached the road there was no sign of Peter either. His head jerked one way and then the other. What had happened? Had Potter shot him?

Before his thoughts took him any farther he was made to swing round by the crashing sound and the neighing of a horse, and there in the far distance he saw that Potter had driven his cart into a ditch, and it and the horse were lying on their sides.

He was tearing along the road now, and he had covered half the distance to the cart when he saw Potter staggering up onto the fell with a bundle under his arm. The bundle was no longer struggling but was hanging limply.

"Potter! You, Potter! Drop him. Let him go!"

Potter, casting a glance over his shoulder, now began to run, but being hampered by his burden his progress was slow, and Davy was quickly gaining on him when Potter, stopping abruptly, turned, and his voice brought Davy to a halt, "No farther, or else!" He shook the limp body. "He's not dead yet, but one more peep out of you an' he will be. Come here!"

Slowly Davy moved forward, and when he was within a few yards of Potter, the man said, "Get goin' on in front . . . into the mine."

"What!"

"You heard."

"No, I'll not, I'll not go in there." He glanced sharply about him. Where was Peter?

"Do it now or . . ." As Potter leveled the gun down toward John Willie's head Davy moved slowly forward.

"Put a move on. Hurry. Run. Go on, run."

Davy ran, but slowly, glancing over his shoulder all the while, and his glance swept the fell just before he entered the mouth of the mine. But there wasn't a soul to be seen.

Potter was close behind him now, and he too turned and scanned the fell. Then on the sound of a weary "Huh! Huh!" he said, "So you've come round. Then stand on your feet. Up with you!"

Davy stopped and turned and saw John Willie standing swaying, while Potter held him by the collar. There was a cut on his temple, and a trickle of blood was running down his cheek. The sight of it caused a blind anger to rise in Davy, and without thinking of the consequences he was about to spring forward when the nozzle of the pistol was thrust almost into his face.

"Back with you or I'll blow your face in! Go on, back, back!"

Davy backed; he backed until the light became dim and Potter and John Willie were just silhouettes against it. Then Potter's voice came to him, hissing now, "Stand still, just where you are, an' keep quiet. One peep out of you and I'll let you have it. And he'll go along of you."

Potter's words seemed to indicate to Davy that he wasn't going to shoot them out of hand; if that was his intention he could have done so before now. Yet the next minute he fired the gun.

Davy had a blurred vision of John Willie gripping Potter's leg; there was a squeal of pain; then Potter kicked out at John Willie and sent him flying, and at the same instant the gun went off. The sound was still reverberating along the shaft when there came to Davy's ears the known and ominous rumbling of a roof fall, the snapping of timbers, the groans of stone being released from centuries of pressure, the wrenching, tumbling, terrifying cascade of rock falling from one level to another.

He did not run but stood fixed in fear, every muscle of his back pressed tight against the wall of the roadway. He could see nothing; he was in black total darkness. No debris had fallen near him, but his mouth and nostrils were clogged with dust.

Long after the rumble had died away he remained still; he seemed unable to move from the wall; it was as if he had been nailed there by the blast. Then in the blackness the silence began to yell at him, and his mind began to panic. He was locked in the pit again. But this time he was alone, and no one knew that he was here. They wouldn't think of Potter forcing them into the mine. They would imagine he had made for the town and that he, Davy, had gone after him. And Peter wouldn't be there to suggest looking in the mine, for Peter must have been shot or else he would have been at the corner.

His mother used to say everybody's death was already written down in heaven. His must have read: Davy Halladay will meet his death in the pit, and his brother an' all.

John Willie!

His body was released from the wall. His hands now began to grope frantically along it, and he was amazed at the distance he had to walk before he was brought to a halt by scattered rocks and splintered pit props. He bent down now and felt his way among the mounting debris that formed a wall and hemmed in the roadway. He moved carefully, knowing that were he to dislodge any part of the obstruction it might bring down further parts of the roof on his head. No miner messed about with a roof fall unless he had a light and could see what he was doing. But he could tap, and keep on tapping, in the hope that someone—perhaps Miss Peamarsh—would think about the mine and come to see if they were there.

As his hands groped about in search of a small piece of rock, they came in contact with a curiously shaped object. When his fingers traced its outline he gave an inward gasp. It was a boot, a man's boot; and when his hand, moving upward, touched a woolen sock and a section of bare flesh, he shuddered from head to foot. It was Potter. He was buried under the fall. And with him John Willie! . . . His stomach heaved; he was going to be sick.

He was sick. He half lay, half knelt on the stones and vomited.

John Willie. Oh, John Willie. When he began to cry he did nothing to prevent the tears from spraying down his face. He didn't care now if he never got out; it was as his mother had said, your names have been written down by God. Yet in that case, why had He let them meet up with Miss Peamarsh and take her loneliness away? Because now she'd be more lonely than ever without them, even being free from Potter.

. . . What was that?

. . . There it was again, a faint sound, like somebody whispering at the far end of a tunnel. . . . It was somebody talking. He turned onto his knees and, grabbing up a stone, knocked it three times against another. Then scarcely breathing, he waited. . . . One, two, three. There came the answer.

He stood up now and shouted, "I'm here! I'm here!" Faintly now the voice came to him. "Stay quiet. We'll soon have you out. I'm going for help."

He felt faint, dizzy; he was going to pass out. But no, he wasn't going to do that. Who ever heard of anybody fainting with relief? A minute ago he had wanted to die because John Willie was gone, now he was glad he was going to live. What was the matter with him?

Oh my, he felt bad. Funny, he couldn't get his breath. . . . And then he knew the reason why. There was no air. Yet the roadway stretched back to the ventilation shaft, the one he had called up, the one he had lain under that awful night. It came to his fuddled thinking that there must have been another fall sometime previously. There were roof falls all the time in the old workings, for the roof props were rotten.

How long could he last out? He must lie flat; that's what the pitmen did when trapped: they lay flat.

He groped his way back over the scattered rocks until he came to the bogey rails, and slowly he lay down between them, and as he lay he began to sweat like he used to do when working in a low wet coal seam. His chest began to heave and a deep heavy tiredness assailed him. His last thought was, would he find their John Willie straightaway when he died, or would God have already sent him on to some special place for the deaf and dumb?

The air was cool on his face. It was cool in his throat; it was pushing out his chest.

"You're all right, lad; you're all right."

He knew that was Peter's voice although he hadn't opened his eyes. He felt so very tired.

"He'll never be nearer death again."

That was Mr. Cartwright. Where had he come from? The answer was given by another voice: "It was nothing short of an act of providence, Mr. Cartwright, that you were on the road and could come to Mr. Talbot's assistance."

"Well, I suppose you could say it was something like that, Miss Peamarsh, but it was another act of providence that it was only a slight fall, so to speak, an' we were quickly through. But it was heavy enough to do for Potter. And it's just as well he went that way from the bit I've gathered, miss. The little 'un only missed it by inches. . . ."

. . . John Willie.

"It's all right; lie still."

He felt himself lifted upward and was vaguely aware he was being carried on a door. He tried to rise. . . . "John Willie."

A hand caught his, and Miss Peamarsh's voice said soothingly, "John Willie's all right. His arm is broken and the doctor is seeing to it. He's all right. Breathe deeply. . . deeply."

John Willie was all right . . . he was alive . . . they were both alive.

He breathed deeply.

Twelve

Miss Peamarsh had said the whole affair would die down like a nine days' wonder, and it had.

Davy lay in bed staring up at the rafters through the dying glow of the fire. They had brought the bed into the living room because of John Willie's cough. It was now almost three weeks since they had dragged him for dead out of the mine, and from the following week Davy had seemed to do nothing but answer questions from Justices' clerks and newspapermen. That was when he wasn't stopping folks from climbing the wall to see where the skeleton had been buried. Sunday was the worst day, for this, for then the young lads came from the towns and swelled those already packing the road, whole families who were taking a jaunt and who peered through the iron gates hoping to catch a glimpse of the woman who had been daft enough, as some said, to allow herself to be black-

179

mailed just so that her father's name could remain unblemished.

The second week there were fewer people, for their attention had been caught by the near riot that had ensued when pitmen were being evicted from their homes and the Irish were being installed in them.

Then last week the house had been almost deserted, for Miss Peamarsh had taken to jaunting herself. Almost every day a hired carriage had come to the gates and she had driven away, and wherever she went he knew it had nothing to do with the case, for Potter was buried, and her brother was buried, decently, and now all that remained to be cleared up was the return of the money she had paid to Potter. And the solicitors were seeing to that by selling his shop. So where did she go on her jaunts?

He had, over the past days, felt strangely alone, almost lost. During the first two weeks he had seen a lot of Peter, for he had stayed on by the Justices' request and, like himself, had had to repeat the same things over and over again. In his case, he described how the wily Potter had locked the gate after him and how he'd torn back up the drive again, and Miss Peamarsh had supplied another key from the study. And how all this had taken time. But now he hadn't seen Peter for three days and was under the sad impression that he had gone on his way without saying good-bye to him.

People were funny. All people were funny, Miss Peamarsh funniest of all. As his mother would have said, she was acting like somebody let loose. He had heard the Justice say to her, "Now you can start living." Well, all he could say was she wasn't losing much time. And she had changed. She looked younger, and she acted sprightly like. He didn't think he liked her acting sprightly—he had the niggling idea that she might not need them anymore, not for company like, just for work. Well, that's what he was here for, wasn't it? Aye, but he wanted company. He had said to Peter the last time he had seen him, "I wish in a way I was comin' with you when you go, man," and Peter had punched him in the chest, saying, "Don't be a fool, lad. Be thankful your bread's been buttered; if not for your own sake, then for the nipper's."

And he was thankful. Yes, he was, especially for John Willie's sake. But it was odd about John Willie and the miss, for he had twigged the change in her an' all, and he wasn't happy about it. There was a look on his face as if he knew he was being thrust aside to make way for a new interest.

Aw, he'd better go to sleep; he had work to do the morrow. That's what he was here for, wasn't it, to work? That's what she paid him three shillings a week for, wasn't it? It was no wage, but it was either that or the road, or with luck a job down the pit again. What was he saying, with luck a job down the pit? The next time he found himself down a pit he knew he really would die. Third time catchy time. The very thought of the pit brought him out in a sweat as it had done every day since he had been rescued, both in daylight and during sleep.

He now began to gabble a confused prayer, the essence of which was he wouldn't mind working for three shillings a week for the rest of his life as long as he wasn't forced to go into a mine again.

The following morning, at ten o'clock prompt, he escorted Miss Peamarsh to the gate as he had done every morning that week, and there as usual she turned to him and said, "I shall be returning about four o'clock. There is plenty of food on the dresser. See that John Willie eats all his dinner. Neither of you appeared to have eaten much yesterday." And now she stood staring at him while her eyes moved over his face. She was looking at him, he thought, like someone who was going away and not coming back. He felt all churned up, sickly like. Something was up. What, he just didn't know. But his stomach told him it augured no good for him and John Willie.

"If Mr. Talbot should call, tell him I'd like to see him before he leaves, will you?"

"Yes, miss." She was likely going to give Peter a little reward for all he had done. Well, he could do with it when he went on the road again. By lad, he'd miss him. He wondered where he had got to.

The day seemed never-ending. To make him more depressed, there was a chilling drizzly rain falling. Toward the end of the afternoon he collected the eggs, locked the hens in after gathering up the strays to prevent the fox dining on another chicken as he had done twice this week, milked Florence, then, having scraped his clogs thoroughly and wiped them on the rope mat, he went into the kitchen, where he had left John Willie and Snuffy, John Willie's job being to keep the fire going, which he did with one hand, for he still carried the other in a sling.

"Huh. Huh." John Willie nodded toward the window, and Davy replied, "Aye, it's almost dark; she should be back by now. I'll light the lamp and the lantern."

He had just placed the candle in the lantern and closed the small door when he heard the gate bell ring.

She had her own key, but she always rang the bell when she arrived.

Signaling to John Willie that he was going to the gate, he hurried out and down the drive. Before he reached it he saw her coming toward him, and when he held the lantern high he noticed immediately yet another change in her; she seemed tired as if she had had an exhausting day, but what was more she seemed very pleased to see him.

"I'm so glad to be home, David," she said as they walked up the drive together. "I don't like towns, much less cities. I have been driven all the way to Newcastle and back today."

"Really, miss, Newcastle! I . . . I thought you were in Shields."

"No, Newcastle. Right to Newcastle and back, David."

"By! that's all of seven miles each way. And you didn't like it?"

"I liked the drive but not the city. It's very grand, of course. I will take you there one day."

"Will you, miss? Eeh! I'd like that. I've been as far as Gateshead but never across the water. Not up that end, though I've been across to North Shields an' up t'other side as far as Willington quay."

"Where is John Willie?"

"In the kitchen, miss. I kept him in out of the rain like you said."

"Good."

When they entered the kitchen she immediately put her hand out toward John Willie, and he ran to her and gripped it with his own small thin one and, looking up at her, gave her a rapid succession of huhs.

She did not immediately take off her outdoor things, but, dropping down onto the settle, she looked at Davy and said, "Will you make me a cup of tea, David, please?"

"Aye, miss. Yes of course."

While he swiftly busied himself making the tea she stood up and took off her hat and coat and handed them to John Willie, and he carried them, as if they were precious vestments, and laid them across the back of a chair.

The tea made, Davy brought the cup to her on a tray, and after saying, "Thank you," she took two sips from it before looking up to him and puzzling him by asking, "Are you very fond of your name?"

"Me name, miss? You mean Davy?"

"No, I mean Halladay."

"Aye, miss; well, it's the only name I've got." He grinned at her.

"How would you like another name, David, another surname?"

"Surname, miss? I . . . I don't quite get you, follow you, I mean."

"Come, sit down. Bring that chair and sit opposite to me, here."

When he was seated looking at her where she sat bending slightly toward him, one arm hugging John Willie to her, she said, "What do you think I've been doing these past days?"

"I . . . I couldn't really say, miss, except talking to the Justices about getting your money back from Potter's missis." He could have added, "Enjoying yourself, living, like the Justice said," but he didn't.

"Yes, I've been talking to the Justices about Potter and my money, but also about something else. I have no family, David. Do you know that? I have no one belonging to me in the wide world, and I was a very lonely woman until you and John Willie came into my life. And now I want you to stay in my life. How would you like to be my family, my real family, take my name, and live in this house with me?"

. . ."Miss." He hardly heard the word himself, it was so lost in wonder. His face screwed up, he gulped, coughed, then muttered, "In the house with you! Be your real family, take your name?"

"That's what I said, David." Her voice was a whisper now. "You could still keep your own; you would be known as David Halladay Peamarsh, and he"—she pulled John Willie tighter toward her—"John William Halladay Peamarsh. . . .That is what I've been doing these past days, talking to the Justice and to a solicitor. And it can all be arranged. That is, if you are agreeable, because you are answerable not only for yourself but for John Willie also."

. . ."Miss," he drew the word out again while he screwed up his eyes tightly. He couldn't take it in. He was listening to her voice as if it were coming from a distance.

"You would be my sons; it would all be done legally."

There was that dreadful feeling coming over him again, that feeling of uncontrollable emotion. He might have conquered it, but at that moment she put out her arms and drew him toward her. It was the first time she had put her arms about him. She had petted and fondled John Willie but had never even held his hand. He couldn't recall what had happened when he had been carried from the mine. He hadn't until this moment been aware of how much he had wanted her to do just that, to hold his hand, put her arms about him. . . . The storm rose and burst. His head against her thin neck, he sobbed, and his crying increased as she stroked his hair, repeating brokenly, "There, there. There, there."

He felt afterward that he might have gone on and on for hours disgracing himself had not the gate bell clanged again. At the sound of it he sheepishly withdrew himself from her and made an attempt to check his weak outburst, as he thought of it, and go to the gate. But she checked him gently, and there was a break in her own voice as she said, "It's all right, my dear; stay where you are; I'll see to it. Come, John Willie."

Through his misted gaze he saw her lift her old cloak from the back of the door and throw it about her shoulders, take up the lantern, then grab John Willie's hand and go out of the kitchen with a step that put him in mind of a young lass hitching.

Alone in the kitchen, he wiped his face roughly with the coarse towel. Eeh! he couldn't believe it. He'd wake up and find he was dreaming. For them to live in here, in this house and be known as her sons! Things like this didn't happen to lads like him; he was a miner's son; only a few months ago he had thought he would have lived and died a miner's son, grubbing away in the bowels of the earth in order to earn enough money to enable him to exist on the top of it, and think himself lucky to be in work. But here he was, going to be adopted by a woman who had once scared the daylights out of him, but who just a minute ago had put her arms about him and hugged him like a real mother would. He faced the lonely fact that his own mother had never hugged him, nor could he remember her ever kissing him. The only affection he had really known had come from John Willie, and the only love John Willie had known had come from himself. There had been no time for love and soft feelings in their family. But now he seemed enveloped in it, both he and John Willie; it would take time to get used to. And she had called him "My dear."

The door opened and he turned to see her enter, still holding John Willie by the hand, and behind her, standing in the doorway, was Peter. He watched him drop the sling of blankets and pans from his shoulder onto the doorstep, then come into the kitchen.

"Mr. Talbot has come to say good-bye, David."

"Aw, you're goin' then, Peter?"

"Yes, yes, I'm ready for the road, lad. But straightaway I want to say that I'm delighted to hear the latest news. The miss here has just been telling me."

Davy's head drooped slightly and he shook it as he said softly, "I can't take it in, not yet." Then he lifted his glance and looked to where Miss Peamarsh was now busying herself between the table and the dresser. Then her voice, which now held a faint resemblance to that of the old Miss Peamarsh he remembered, was saying, "Stir the fire, David, and get the kettle to boil quickly. Mr. Talbot could, I think, do with a cup of tea. Is that right, Mr. Talbot?" She cast a glance over her shoulder toward Peter, and he answered, after a slight pause, "That's right, miss; it would be very acceptable."

"Please sit down."

Peter sat down, and Davy stirred the fire briskly, and he was hanging the kettle on the hook above it when he was brought swiftly about as again Miss Peamarsh's voice reminded him of days gone by, for she was saying, "Well!" with the old imperious tone. "Well! Mr. Talbot, I have a proposal to make to you. That is, a business proposal."

"Really, miss! You have a proposal to make to me?"

Davy seemed to detect a note of laughter in Peter's voice, and he wanted to say to him, "Eeh! don't joke with her like that, man, or she'll get vexed." But Miss Peamarsh seemingly was not taking the remark amiss, for she repeated, "That is what I said, a proposal." Then she paused before going on, "This is a very small estate, only fourteen acres of land, but at one time there was a good orchard, a fine vegetable garden, and enough grazing for a couple of cows, and chickens in plenty. What I propose to do is to bring it back to its former state. Now David, although he is a strong boy, could not possibly achieve this on his own, and what is more, in the future, half his day will be taken up with study. . . . Yes, yes, that is a surprise to you." She laughed openly now at the look on Davy's face. Then turning to Peter again, she said, "What I am proposing, Mr. Talbot, is to offer you a post here. I cannot place a heading to it, and say it is to be gardener, or handyman, or joiner, or the glorified title of steward, for you will, I am afraid, should you accept, be called upon to turn your hand to anything and everything that you find necessary. . . . Well, there you have it, that is my proposal. But before you accept, or refuse, I must tell you that I cannot afford to pay you a really large wage, although I now have full use of my income and may in due course recover my past losses. I am still not and never will be even a moderately rich woman, and because of this I propose, when the place is put to rights, to go into business, the business of a small farm or market garden. So all I offer you at present by way of a wage would be eight shillings a week; this together with your food and your house, the one David occupies now. . . . Well, there it is. What do you say, Mr. Talbot?"

Some twenty seconds passed before Peter spoke. He wetted his lips a number of times before he answered her, and then his voice came from deep in his throat as he said, "Would a drowning man refuse a rope, miss? And the one you are holding out is plaited with silver. At the moment I'm stumped for words. My faith in human nature has been wearing thin of late, but now—well, as I said, miss, what can I say by way of thanks? Only time will prove how I feel at this moment."

As he stared at her and she at him, Davy looked from one to the other. There was a strange quiet pervading the room until John Willie, slipping down from the form, ran to Peter, and, looking up at him with his great brown eyes laughing and his mouth wide, he emitted a great loud "HUH."

The sound was so expressive that they burst out laughing, and Davy laughed louder than any of them, because he knew that if he didn't he'd make a fool of himself again.

"What was he trying to tell me?" Peter now looked at Davy, and Davy said, "I think he was saying that he's glad you're stayin'. And . . . and that goes for me an' all, Peter."

"Thank you, lad. By, it's strange to think that if I hadn't bumped into you in the workhouse that day none of this would have happened. I'm standing here now because of that."

"Huh. Huh. Huh." John Willie was now giving voice to a rapid string of huhs; then he dived to the corner of the hearth where Snuffy lay curled in the place that he had claimed as his own, and getting down beside him he put his arms around his neck and raised his head. Then looking from one to the other of them, he again gave voice to a rapid series of huhs.

Davy, after staring at him for a moment, emitted the sound himself. "Huh!" he said. "Well I never! You know what he's pointin' out, miss?" He turned to Miss

Peamarsh. "He's tellin' us that the one who should be given the credit for the good fortune that has fallen on him, and me, and Peter here, is because of Snuffy . . . I mean Rex."

Miss Peamarsh turned and looked down at the small boy hugging the shaggy dog and said softly, "Yes, indeed, indeed." But it was John Willie she was referring to when she added, "He has more common sense in his little head than all of us put together. And he will be a great help to us as he grows older." Then, her eyes blinking, she swallowed deeply before adding, "Come now, come now, we must eat. And this must be a special meal, a special tea, for it happens to be my birthday."

She smiled from one to the other, and Peter said, "May I wish you many more of them, miss?" and she replied, "Thank you, Mr. Talbot." But Davy said nothing; he just stared at her. It was her birthday and she had given everybody so much, him especially, and to his mind she was getting very little in return. If he only had something to give her, just some little thing. But he had, he had: the jug. Aye, the jug.

He startled them by turning round and dashing out of the room. Bounding across the dark yard, he ran up the black well of the stairs, whipped up the jug from the mantelpiece and was back in the kitchen within a matter of minutes, and there, panting, he held it out to her.

Slowly Miss Peamarsh's hands lifted toward him, and when they covered his and the jug she said brokenly, "Oh, David, David, to give me the only thing of value you possess."

Their gaze held for a moment before he could say, "I've got everything, miss; you've given us everything, everything we'll ever want, yourself, an' your name.

But you've done something more for me. You've made it possible for me to see daylight all me life. I need never worry about going below again."

And now it was he who put his arms about her and held her, and it was Miss Peamarsh who cried, and unashamedly.